TRIALS OF THE VAMPIRE

A Witch Between Worlds: Book #2

EMMA GLASS

I

ELLIOTT

The longer Clara Blackwell remained comatose in a medical bed, the deeper I felt myself fall into an inconsolable depression. Silently, I watched her through the glass and reflected on my mistakes.

The protection spell was used with the best of intentions, I heard the reminder in the back of my head. *Clara was in grave danger. Vampires have an insatiable hunger for human blood – you've felt it yourself. You have seen what it does to even the friendliest of people...*

And someone had already come looking for her.

But the spell backfired—badly.

There was no telling what really happened. One minute, she was fine if not horribly confused; the next, everything seemed to go utterly wrong.

My wrath had no proper outlet. Without the truth, there was no clear person or circumstance to blame. There were simply just too many factors in play. The problem could've been the spell itself, the sorceress casting it, the unstable conditions, outright sabotage, or even...

My eyes closed with grief.

I could still feel that coursing wind that held me at bay that night. I remembered how hard it was to take one horrified step after another, pushing myself forward to desperately reach her.

You interrupted the magic, Elliott. Maybe you yourself are just as much to blame...

There were no answers.

That was the worst part.

There is always an answer, logic dictated. But here I stood, blindly grasping at straws. All the while, the one I'd meant to save remained on a medical bay bed – suspended in a deep, magical sleep that none of us could even pretend to understand.

"How?" Asking nobody in particular, I firmly planted my palms against the windowpane and lowered my head in sinking despair. "*How* could this have happened?"

A voice approached. "It's simple, really."

I glanced up. The regal, aloof woman that I reluctantly called a *mother* strolled casually down the hall towards me. My disposition soured at the very sight of her. "We were all there, Elliott. It was—"

"*Rhetorical*," I snapped an annoyed glance at Lorelei Craven. "It was *rhetorical*."

My mother folded her arms, turning away in faint disinterest. "You were never of a particularly *patient* mind, Elliott—and in that impatience, you turned to dangerous and unproven magic." She tilted her head curiously. "How, then, could you be surprised that *this* is the fruit you must reap?"

I hated that she barely cared.

I hated even more that she was right.

"Clara's life was endangered," I reminded her. Yet I could barely convince even *myself* that I'd been right to rush ahead with what she rightfully called 'unproven magic.' *But I'm not about to tell her that—she seems to get angrier not when I make a mistake, but when I admit it...* "What would you have had me do instead?"

"You have always been a creature of logic, my son. *Desperation* doesn't suit you. Why you chose now to try it on for size, I have no idea." Lorelei turned to the glass. "That desperation might have killed her. It's likely we won't know for sure until some time has passed – when she's either woken back up, or dropped dead."

While true, the observation only twisted the knife. My forehead slowly lowered to the window, and I sank further into bleak despair. Had I been of right mind, I wouldn't have ever dreamed of letting the words fall from my lips.

"You've failed me lately."

The change in the air was immediate. I heard a small, accusatory hiss seep from her crimson lips, but there was no going back now.

"*Every* time that I've asked you for advice this past year, you have feigned disinterest..." I pried myself from the glass with mounting anger. "You want to abdicate the throne? Fine, I'll pick up the slack. You want to thrust it into my unprepared hands? Then 'trial by fire' it is."

I took a few menacing steps closer.

"But you've done *nothing* to guide me, *nothing* to teach me. You offer me no support, only your constant criticism." I glared into her eyes, forcing her to turn away. "You were never like this before. You're like a stranger to me now. *How* have you so radically changed?"

For a brief moment, a flicker of regret crossed Lorelei's face. But then came the aloof haze that I hated so much, washing away any accountability from her expression.

Fine. If you'll be no help to me...

"Leave me," I growled.

She couldn't even be bothered to argue.

Without so much as another glance at Clara's

comatose body in the medical bay, Lorelei Craven apathetically sauntered back down the hallway.

※

THE DOOR QUIETLY CLICKED BEHIND ME AS I STEPPED back into the room, observing the six vampires I'd hand-picked to save Clara Blackwell.

I had to be near her again.

Vampires had little need of medical staff, not with our regenerative systems. But the rulers of the Eight Holds, myself included, lived firmly in the public eye. With our stations of power, it was unreasonable to chance a coup leaving a lingering wound, or even a simple untreated mishap. Thus, we kept some of the most qualified professionals in the world at our employ, serving in our castles.

The two best nurses in Stonehold were here on the Isle of Obsidian, constantly tending to the human in our care. Clara's vital signs beeped over a few antiquated machines as they carefully kept an eye on her. This was almost a formality, as I didn't honestly expect them to be particularly useful to the cause. The nurses and their devices were used to vampire anatomy, after all.

Furthermore, nobody was fooled here. We all knew Clara's unnatural rest was the direct result of powerful magic gone awry, something beyond the skill and scope of purely medical expertise.

Speaking of the Devil...

My gaze shifted to the sorceress. The newest visitor to my castle kept herself buried in the very spellbook she'd used to perform the spell. In an act of implied selflessness, the exotic Sabine was insistent on remaining near Clara, determined to find a way to bring her back to us.

Even with only fleeting interactions with her, I sense more to Sabine. I called upon a powerful caster from the mainland — looks like I've gotten one. But I can't help but wonder why she offers her services so freely...

She hadn't asked for anything; Sabine arrived in the castle with little more than meager supplies and a demonstration of her power. But dismissing her left only one other nearby vampire capable of discovering the truth: Sebastian, the elderly sage deep down in the castle libraries. Already, I had the old man digging in the ancient literature. The tragedy had shaken him, for it was *he* who found the spell in the first place...

Perhaps I'm wrong, I reasoned. *If she truly acts in compassion, then Sabine is right to prioritize the danger over the perceived rewards.* It was foolish, I know, but there was a part of me that didn't want her anywhere *near* Clara.

The nurses kept glancing distractedly at the other three in the room, perched together nearby. Clara's chosen guardians were formerly royal guards of mine that she'd personally picked to protect her: the ever-cheerful jokester Wilhelm, his peaceful and brooding partner Viktor, and the sensible yet blunt Asarra. I'd ordered the three of them to remain present here, in case any of the others gave into the legendary bloodlust that vampires held for human beings.

Even Wilhelm was uncharacteristically grim. Since Clara's collapse, I hadn't seen so much as a smirk cross his usually jovial face. If nothing else, his change in attitude reassured me that he was taking it seriously. *If Wilhelm of all people can't bring himself to crack a joke, then I can trust the others to work themselves to the bone over Clara...*

Between the six of them, I truly felt that my adoring, otherworldly guest was in good hands.

I just hoped it would be enough.

※

THE OTHERS BARELY ACKNOWLEDGED MY PRESENCE AS I checked on Clara. *Good,* I thought to myself. *I should be an afterthought in this room.*

Standing over her with a heavy heart, I lightly tilted my chin towards one of her Knightly Trio. Solemn, thoughtful Viktor blinked to attention at my motion, still conditioned to serve his liege.

"Have there been any changes?" I asked.

"None, Lord Elliott," he answered dutifully. "Clara sleeps peacefully as ever. Not so much as a fitful twist or a roll out of this one. She rests just as calmly as we guards do."

Viktor referred, naturally, to the treatments royal guards were given during their training. One of their gained talents was a deep and restful pause they could activate or dispel at will. When he or she so chose, a royal guard could slip into a statuesque sleep to allow time to pass while they upheld their duties. Being former guards, the three guardians held that ability still.

I folded my arms wearily. "This couldn't have *possibly* happened at a worst time. News from the chrysm mines grows bleaker by the day." I turned to the guardian with a hint of irritation. "Soon, it will be expected for me to depart the castle and tend to the problem in person."

His companions shared a meaningful look.

"You're leaving?" Wilhelm asked.

My eyes trailed to the comatose girl. I took a step towards her and warmly stroked away a few stray strands of her hair. She looked so serene in her slumber – just as always in the fortnight that I'd spent waking up beside her.

"It's the last thing I want to do right now. But the needs of the people tie my hands. If what Silas tells me is true…" I lightly stroked my knuckles against her rosy, flush cheek. With a small smile, I tried to memorize the tranquility across her face, so elegantly painted and composed. Reluctantly, I glanced back up at Clara's bodyguard.

"I could have a full-scale revolt on my hands. I don't need to remind you that our entire planet is dependent on the stuff – especially *our* reserves. If our chrysm harvest halts, we could stand at the brink of worldwide pandemonium."

The room was silent. I realized that everyone was watching me, and I grunted with annoyance. "I can't delay the inevitable any longer. The entire point of our spell was to ensure her safety while I was tending to this disaster. It's already been two days... I can't avoid my responsibilities as ruler of Stonehold any longer. I'm needed off the island."

Wilhelm narrowed his eyes. The expression was one that I immediately hated. "With all due respect, Lord Elliott... you've ignored the pleas of your boring old chancellor for as far back as I can remember. Since when did you start caring about your *responsibilities?*"

Every pair of eyes focused on us.

"Since my time with Clara has shown me the lack of confidence my people have in my reign," I replied coolly. "Case in point, *that* outburst. The *only* reason I'm not having you severely punished for that remark is the stress this situation puts us both under."

I leaned forward with a look of pure malice. *If my*

subjects are this willing to speak out against me, particularly after only a single year in my reign...

"Wilhelm, you above most others understand my thoughts on insubordination. If it wasn't for your obvious care towards your human charge – and that I know you speak only in her defense – I'd happily relieve some of my crippling stress by *personally* whipping your back bloody."

Wilhelm's defiance evaporated in a heartbeat. I had never threatened one of my own subjects in such a way before, and the thought of it made my stomach turn. But the inexplicable arrival of a mythological creature on my world, and a *human being* at that, forced me to do a number of things I'd never done before.

Satisfied at his silence, I addressed the group. "Your orders remain. As far as any of you are to be concerned, *Clara* is my priority right now. Protect her while I'm stuck solving the damned problems on the mainland."

The six of them respectfully nodded together. Even Sabine, the relative newcomer that she was, seemed devotedly committed to the cause, despite my thoughtful suspicions.

Innocent until shown otherwise...

"Good," I noted appreciatively. "Now, I'll leave you all to it. Keep her stable, keep her safe... and *find a goddamn way to save her.*"

With that order, I turned to leave. I only made it a

few strides away before the weight in my core tugged my boots to a complete stop. *No,* I decided. *There's still something I have to do first...*

They looked surprised as I walked back to the comatose human's side. Quickly bending over her slumbering body, I planted my lips to hers.

Come back to me, Clara, I urged her.

I need you.

2
CLARA

While my body slept faraway in a world full of vampires that lusted for my blood, my mind was elsewhere. In a distant land that felt like a distant dream, I walked alongside my grandmother.

In her company, I spent some time admiring the crisp waves and how they continuously rolled against the soft sand. *But this isn't a dream at all, is it?* I thought as I basked in the sounds of the soothing sea breeze, and how it whipped in from over the ocean. Even if I couldn't feel the salty air on my skin or the lapping water against my toes, the striking tropical sights didn't suffer.

At any rate, this wasn't like any dream that I'd had before. Even the recurring nightmares that had plagued me for weeks – so familiar to me by now – had nothing on my clarity here. While I usually dreamt in half-formed details, the world here felt as real as the vampiric world – and as the world I'd been calling home for seventeen years.

"Come," she pointed towards a nearby trail in the treeline, one I could have sworn wasn't there just moments before. "The ocean is beautiful, yes, but where we're going requires less distraction."

As Grandma strolled forward with her cane, her bohemian clothes and gypsy jewelry fluidly moved around her body. It was buffeted by a gust of wind that I only barely felt. It was just another reminder of the reality of my situation: *No matter how realistic this all is, I'm not really here with her.*

Sand still trailed up the slight incline into the jungle. As the crashing waves receded quietly into the background, I realized that the jungle around us stood completely still and silent. Without the slightest hint of wildlife, this entire place felt like it was somehow just for us.

In a way, maybe it was.

EITHER SECONDS OR EONS LATER, WE WERE FURTHER UP the trail. The sand faded to dirt; the surrounding jungle thickened to the point of near darkness on either side of our path.

I realized that my elderly guide was observing me from the corner of her eye, just as silent as the trees around us. While I wondered how long she'd been watching me for a reaction, a small smirk lit up her face.

"Tell me, Clara... what you see?"

"Everything is grayscale," I observed quietly. "There's no colour in the moonlight. Maybe there's just no colour here altogether."

"Perhaps. But perhaps you're just colourblind."

"But... I can *see* colours usually..."

"Can you?" She paused to point the tip of her cane at a nearby palm. "Tell me, then, what colour is the trunk on this tree?"

"Oh." I squinted at the tall, swaying tree. "Um. I don't know. Brown?"

Chuckling, she shook her head. "You *expect* it to be brown because that's what you're used to. After all the things you've seen with your last few weeks, I'd think you might have learned by now."

"Learned what, Grandma?"

"Abandon everything you thought you knew, Clara Blackwell, because from here on out it only holds you back."

I looked at the tree again, lost in thought.

"You have experienced ethereal travel — twice recently, in fact. It perfectly stands to reason that shifting into another world causes things to be, how can

I word this..." Her eye twinkled craftily. "Lost in translation, as it were."

"Like colours," I wondered aloud. I turned back to her curiously. "So, what color's the tree, then?"

"It was a trick question," she smiled impishly. "You were right before. *This* tree has no colour, *that* tree has no colour... nothing in this place has color because there *is* no colour."

I looked at her. "Why?"

"What do you mean, 'why?'"

"Why isn't there colour in this world?"

"Because this isn't a world, per se. At least, not by the conventional definition of the word."

I groaned. "So I *am* dreaming then?"

"Yes and no..." She began walking again, and I followed. "You were *always* dreaming, Clara, but that doesn't make this place any less real than the ones you've already seen," Grandma clarified with a playful glance. "Your mind can exist without the body, so long as the body is kept safe. What you're experiencing here is still actually happening to you, just in a way you've never seen before."

I nodded, considering all of this.

It was a lot for me to process.

"Now then. I enjoy a closed circle just as much as the next old bag," she grinned to me before she repeated herself. "So what do you see, Clara?"

I stopped. "I see..."

She paused, turning to observe me. "Yes?"

"You know, it's taken some getting used to... being here, I mean." My drifting gaze glided across our silent jungle environment; my answer almost came as an afterthought. "Especially the colourless moonlight. Everything I see is in black and white, crisp and clear. It feels like I'm walking through an old photograph. Or maybe a wispy veil of something I don't understand, thinly draping a grayscale filter over my eyes..." I turned to her in a sudden moment of clarity, looking her directly in the eyes. "It's beautiful, all of it."

"Tell me more," she delightedly urged.

"The geography..." My distracted gaze drifted again; I faintly smiled to myself. "I guess growing up in the green heart of the West Midlands hasn't really done me any favours. I don't think I've ever even actually *been* to a beach, not before any of this. Let alone, seeing anything like the sweeping palm trees in the jungle here..."

She watched quietly as I stepped off the sandy trail, idly placing my palm against the thin trunk. Clumped, frizzy fuzz grew up the brittle bark, but I felt nothing. Against my bare skin, the lifelike textures were little more than a hard surface that I couldn't pass my hand through. *Another small casualty of dreaming my way here, I guess.*

Turning my eyes further up the trail, I could see how

it wound deeper into the jungle. The path twisted through the brush, slicing towards a pair of majestic twin peaks. Distantly, they pierced the brilliant night sky with their stretched tips.

"Never seen mountains, either," I continued. "Not outside of movies or watching the telly. But these ones are incredible."

"You seem to be rather enjoying it here."

"It's wonderful!" I nodded fervently. "It's just that... oh, how I wish I could feel the waves on my shins, or enjoy the earthy smells of these hanging coconuts..."

"You understand why you can't, of course."

"Yes." I lowered my head. "I'm asleep."

The elderly bohemian woman gave a small, kind-hearted nod. "That's right, Clara. While your mind is here, your body sleeps in another world."

"You haven't explained how that's possible," I looked at her out of the corner of my eye.

"Explain? Why, what's there to explain?" She chuckled, whacking away a stray branch with her cane. She was leading me into the trees now, off the beaten path. "Your foolhardy friends fiddled with magic far beyond their capabilities. Your body rebelled. You lapsed into a coma, and your mind was left to drift..."

"But it didn't drift, did it?" I asked, following her example. "You said earlier that you brought me here, purposefully." The darkness was parting ahead of us, and we quickly found ourselves on the edge of a cliff, far above placid waves.

My grandmother leaned on her cane, her gaze lazily trailing over the sea. I trailed loosely after it, over the monochromatic ocean under a colorless, starry night sky. I felt in my heart that I stood on the edge of the world here... but this wasn't really a world, and I wasn't really here.

It was enough to make my head hurt.

"Yes," she finally replied, turning to face me. "I brought you here with purpose in mind."

"And why's that?"

"Same reason that spell didn't work on you, or that you were ever able to travel between worlds. For the reason why you've always felt you might be primed for something bigger, something much more than the shoddy life you were handed..."

"Winding up in the vampire world was a total accident," I protested. "A crazy gypsy woman was chasing me! I didn't know what was going on, and I just did what felt right..."

"Of course you did," she nodded caringly. "But what that's just it, Clara. What felt natural to you then... that *separates* you, my child, because that was no, uh – how did you put it?"

"What, the crazy gypsy woman?"

"Ah, yes. That wasn't any mere *'crazy gypsy woman',*"

she chuckled. "No, that woman you met put something into play that was never meant for you. Yet, you inadvertently took it from her."

She laughed at how my expression changed.

"No need to be downtrodden, these things can happen sometimes. But when you met her at *that* moment, things changed forever. You wound up mixed up in powerful things far bigger than you realize that day – things that transcend both your world *and* the one you just left. All because of your heritage, and the truth of your blood."

"My blood? My heritage?" I quizzically shook my head. "Grandma, what are you telling me?"

"Understand that you won't remember any of the things that you learn here," the old, bohemian woman smiled sadly. "The nature of dreaming is that one does not retain the memories gained in their slumber – but your subconscious?"

She tapped a fingertip to my forehead.

"*That* will imprint, and that is how I must prepare you for what is coming. You must learn, Clara, and we don't have the time. So I'll hide the knowledge deep in your mind for you to use when you are finally ready..."

"I don't understand, Grandma."

"It doesn't matter that you don't. Your mind will hold these sleeping memories that I will give you, waiting inside you for when the right time comes. But as a result,

I suspect that anything beyond this point, you will forget as soon as you return to your friends."

"I'll forget meeting you again?"

"It's likely," she shrugged. "But who knows? If we're lucky, I just might get to see you again. Sadly, I doubt such a thing will be for a very long time. But more importantly, for now..."

She smirked knowingly and leaned closer.

"Clara Blackwell... you're a *witch*."

3
ELLIOTT

Atop my throne, I listened to the prattling speech of my elderly high chancellor, Silas. Insufferably boring and tedious, I'd spent the duration of my life strictly avoiding him.

But now that I was the sitting vampire lord of Stonehold, the people's whisperer had become an unfortunate daily necessity to my duties.

"Might I say, Lord Elliott, I'm delighted you're *finally* listening to reason." The thin, bothersome old man stood near the base of the throne stairs, wringing his slender and bony hands. Everything he ever did was composed with an air of haughty exaggeration, and it *seriously* got on my nerves. "My utmost hope is that we aren't acting on this matter far too late…"

Unimpressed, I wearily rolled my eyes. The aftermath

of Clara's spell had kept me exhausted. I was far too tired to deal with him right now.

"When our human guest appeared within the castle, the world didn't screech to an end, Silas. I fully expect our problems over on the mainland to wind up being more of the same." My eyebrow arched disapprovingly. "I trust that you've taken the obligatory measures, yes?"

"Of course, Lord Elliott," he graciously bowed. "I've sent word of your impending arrival to your attendants at the nearest junction. Once you have settled in, you'll meet with the miner's guild to discuss the matters at hand."

"Are they striking?" I asked him pointedly.

Silas wilted under my direct scrutiny. "I... am not entirely sure, I'm afraid. Even *I* struggled to get close enough to unearth the truth, to no avail. One thing is certain, however." Unusual for him, he straightened his back and looked me squarely in the eyes. It's how I knew he was being serious. "Whatever is going on in those mines, my Lord, it is of paramount concern. The hold *cannot* abide these slowdowns any longer."

Leaning back in my throne, I nodded.

"We are in agreement, Silas."

He blinked in surprise. "We are? If I may be so bold, Lord Elliott, I never thought I'd see the day."

It was the first time he'd ever said something that

made me smirk. "That makes twice in a row. You're on a hot streak now."

But I couldn't stay amused for long. I'd told myself for three centuries that the moment Silas and I agreed was a definite sign of the apocalypse. Not only that, but Clara Blackwell's life delicately hung in the balance – and I was being forced to leave her side, made to settle some petty squabble that could jeopardize the entire world.

Maybe we'll get that apocalypse after all...

AN HOUR LATER, IN THE COMPANY OF SIX VETERAN royal guards, I finally stepped on a teleportation node.

Brilliantly glowing crimson in chrysm light, the circular platform acknowledged its master's presence by quickly thrumming to life. A column of bright red light shot up from the node, bathing my entourage and me in soothing luminescence.

Within the blink of an eye, we were instantly halfway across the castle, standing together on another node.

I descended the stairs with my guards in tow and left the semicircle of nodes. When my mother had spearheaded the chrysm initiative, she'd had upwards of thirty node pairs installed within the castle. Half of the set was here in the chrysm hub, divided into five separated groups to keep energy overloads at a minimum. Their sister nodes were scattered around the castle at strategic points.

But Lorelei Craven, in her tactical expertise, had ordered a DNA lock over the entire network. The nodes never activated without a member of the Stonehold royal family nearby; the two of us alone had complete and unrestricted access to the castle, moving unimpeded at our own whim.

When I led the guards through the dark and narrow passage to the main chrysm hub, with its gigantic screens and vertical machinery, I realized that I'd forgotten a small exception to that rule.

Nikki Craven, my deranged and erratic sister, stood near the two chrysm attendants. *Oh right. In all the trouble lately, I hadn't remembered that she returned recently... what an unwelcome sight.* With a mischievous look in her eyes, she gave me a meaningful glance as I held out an arm to stop my guards.

"Give me a moment," I ordered them.

She met me halfway; we quietly stepped aside into the shadows. Even with our advanced night sight, so much of this large, hulking chamber was drowned in darkness.

"You know, I constantly forget you wandered back at all," I observed coolly. "I suppose a century apart will do that for you..."

Nikki stuck out her tongue.

"Well, little sister, you have my attention..." I sternly folded my arms across my chest. "Unless you weren't planning to tell me *why* you're down here, sulking around in my way?"

Her eyes flashed sadistically.

"Oh, I just wanted to see you off, in case this was the last time I saw you for a while..."

My eyebrow arched. "Why would it be?"

Nikki pulled herself closer from the shadows; her eyes gleamed with a twisted glint. "These are dark and dangerous times, Elliott. You are leaving the castle at a pivotal moment, and..." Her wide, demented grin faltered. "I'm worried about you."

I laughed. "You're *worried?*"

"You sound surprised, brother."

Truth be told, I didn't understand these little mood swings of hers. In our many years apart, it seemed that her insanity had only deepened – and I still didn't trust her, not after the things she had done. *Certainly not after what first drove her from the castle in the first place,* I thought to myself.

But she was still my sister. Her unpredictable nature made her an utter liability, and there was just enough truth tucked behind those heartless, idle threats she loved to make that rightfully concerned anyone in earshot, but... *her moments of lucidity, no matter how brief, prove Nikki Craven is still quite a formidable friend to have.*

I placed a hand on her shoulder.

"I need you right now," I told her truthfully. "The Isle of Obsidian is being left in our mother's care, but she clearly doesn't want the task. I doubt she'll even lift a finger while I'm on the mainland. Please be my eyes and ears during my time away. If necessary..." I winced to even say the words, "If you truly *have* to, take charge."

Nikki stared into my eyes thoughtfully. Deep down inside her, I could see insanity clutching at the fringes of her mind. But my sister valiantly held a straight face and nodded placidly.

"What about your human?"

"You leave her *alone*," I insisted darkly.

My sister tilted her head and lost the battle as her eyes turned slightly deviant. "Oh? Why, she's not using all of that blood inside her... wouldn't it be a downright shame to waste such a perfectly good reservoir? I won't even bleed her dry..."

I dug my fingers into her shoulder deeper. In a lot of ways, pain seemed to be the only language she understood.

"Do you think that hurts?" She grinned.

"No, but I think it gets your attention."

Nikki smirked, but her eyes told me I had it. "Fine. I'll *behave*, and I'll leave the girl alone..."

"I'm glad we could reach an understanding." My grip on her shoulder slowly released. "Watch the castle, keep an eye on our mother dearest, and stop threatening to murder half the servants."

"What?" She politely feigned ignorance. "I haven't done anything of the sort!"

"Nikki, you've been here half a week, and I've already got complaints pouring in from the staff over you." I took a stern step closer. "*Please* don't make my job any harder than it needs to be."

She lowered her gaze.

"Fine. I'll try to keep myself under control."

A half-smile crossed my lips. *You're a liability, but at least you know it... Just hold yourself together for me a little longer, Nikki, please...*

"When I said I needed you, I meant it," I tried to reassure her. "The night you arrived, you told me that war was coming to the world. Whether or not it has anything to do with our sudden guest, there's no denying the danger in the other holds. Sooner or later, I'm going to have to deal with the other vampire lords..."

"That's true," she replied calmly. "We're in an era of peace. They're growing restless."

"One has *already* stepped foot on this island, searching for Clara." I remembered the recent and unexpected arrival of the oldest, most dangerous of my brethren – Akachi Azuzi, smug ruler of the Falvian Badlands to the south. "It's only a matter of time before the vampire lords convene again... and when before that happens, I'll have to rely on you for the things you've learned off this island..."

My sister did something unexpected then: she pulled me into a long and heartfelt embrace.

"Take care of yourself, Elliott." She released me, holding me at arm's length. "Come back to me in one piece. When you've gotten the mines back on track, we have much to discuss."

I nodded solemnly. "I'll be fine."

"Good," she spoke unsteadily. "I believe you."

I summoned the guards and walked over to the nearest spread of chrysm nodes. With folded arms and a reluctant, heavy heart, I stepped onto the teleporter node for the Dawning Mines.

My eyes stayed on her as the node hummed to life under my boots. She gave a small wave with a saddened look plastered across her face.

'I believe you,' she said...

It wasn't like Nikki Craven to lie to me.

THE HEAVY, CONSTRAINING DARKNESS OF THE CHRYSM hub instantly blinked away; in its place now stood the hardy cavern walls of our discreet exit point, hidden in the mountains.

Looming powerfully at our backs thrummed the

chrysm machine that solely lent its energy to the two-way node. As were all the mainland-side node engines, it was a self-regulating design that required only the slightest maintenance – and we had a specialist that checked it once every decade.

With my guards flanking, I stepped outside to confront the dizzying snowcapped peaks on the horizon. Forested hills formed a rolling carpet at the feet of the mountains; sprawled out far below us and within their secluded, rocky heart laid the Dawning Mines. This mountain range dominated the southern edges of Stonehold, impeding access to the two major peninsulas on the other side – but it offered beautiful vistas and remarkable sights seen nowhere else in the world...

"It's beautiful," I heard a guard murmur.

"Yes," I noted dryly. "Yes, it is."

When I was an impressionable young child, Lorelei told me bedtime stories of a great, ancient empire, spreading far from the peninsulas behind these peaks. In her tales, they were had ruled this entire hold for more than a thousand years; their glorious, bloodthirsty civilization was a powerful one that heralded steadfast fighters, remarkable military might, and the finest intellectuals in the entire world.

In the end, their then-unrecognizable society lay in shambles; it had slowly crumbled beneath their own unparalleled hubris and decadence. The world moved on without them and, even through gradual reinvention, they couldn't hold together strong enough to become anything more than forgotten dust in the wind. In fact, the world moved on so far that no record at all of their existence was left—outside of a young child's bedtime stories.

Apparently, they were called the Roman Empire.

Tales and nothing more, I told myself.

Still, while recognizing the military civilization of legend as nothing more than youthful fantasies, that didn't mean I couldn't learn from the tale.

Their fate will never be ours, I insisted.

"My Lord," one of the guards pointed.

My gaze averted to an approaching vampire in a mining transport vehicle, driving up the path lining our mountain. Upon closer inspection, the massive drill attached to the front told a slightly different story for its usual use.

It arrived quickly. Once it parked nearby, our guide climbed from the cockpit in rudimentary worker's garb. He looked to be of middle age with thick, ginger hair. His face was youthful, but he turned to us with eyes that betrayed at least five or six hundred years to him. *Likely long overdue for another equinox,* I recognized. *He'll begin aging again any year now...*

"Lord Craven!" He walked right up to us and gave a quick, perfunctory bow. With less than a year below my belt as the reigning vampire lord, these gestures still made me a tad uncomfortable. "Forgive me for not being ready in time, I didn't realize you'd be here so soon! It'd be an honour to escort you to the village."

My eyebrow arched. *An honour, you say? Silas, that ancient windbag, has made me no stranger to exaggeration...* I was well aware that my rule was nowhere *near* solidified in the eyes of the people, but there was nothing to gain by arguing him.

"We weren't waiting for long," I responded coolly. "But my time here is very limited. Pressing matters at the castle still require my attention. I'm eager to get this all over with."

"Oh?" Such a welcoming expression at first, but it briefly clouded. The shadow disappeared as quickly as it'd come. "A shame then, that. Some of us had hoped to give you a tour of the beautiful scenery out here. As I'm to understand it, you've only once been to the Alpine Ridge."

"They are quite pretty," I spared a glance over his shoulder. "Perhaps another time."

"Pretty much the only thing we've got to keep us all sane out here," he chuckled. "Well, if you're in a hurry, let's get you down to the others. But it's fair to warn you..." He gave me a cheerful but meaningful look. "You might be here longer than you think."

My mood soured, but I remained silent.

Let us hope not...

⁂

WHILE I JOINED HIM IN THE COCKPIT, THE GUARDS climbed into the back. He primed the engines and studied his dashboard readings; once done with the necessary checks, the drilling vehicle lurched into motion, and we were all on our way down to the nearest village.

Even with the size of the engine necessary to move a vehicle like this, it was yet quiet enough to hold conversation. The drill's inactivity certainly played a large part in that. "You know who I am," I noted, "but I don't recall your name."

"Pavric," the vampire miner cheekily grinned, turning us down the steep path back towards the mine. "Pavric Le Varrise, stonemason and master miner to Gransome Village, at your service!"

"Pavric," I repeated, feeling out the syllables. "I know the Le Varrise name... doesn't that make you a descendent of Veric Le Varrise?"

"I'm impressed you recognize it, Lord Craven. Veric was my great grandfather. He's a downright legend in these parts, since discovering the mines and settling the Alpine Ridge."

"If memory serves, he was rather advanced in age when that happened."

"That's right. Veric was in his twilight years. Must've been well over eight hundred years old," he proudly replied. "He broke first ground on the Dawning Mines, got his team in place, secured the family legacy, and dropped from an affliction of the toiling years not long after."

"The toiling years?"

"Slang," he smiled. "It's what we call a case of growing too worn to keep the old ticker running." He turned, tapping meaningfully on his temple. "Blasted thing just quits out of spite."

Nodding, I diverted my attention towards the rising hills against the foot of the mountains. "It really *is* beautiful out here. I should come out to the mainland more often."

"You ain't kidding!" Pavric cheerily whistled, turning the wheel hard and navigating us around a sharp kink along the mountain's side. "Certainly a sight for sore eyes, that's for damn sure."

I agreed silently, watching the cliff-side trail twist and turn down towards the open mines. The sun was setting in the distance; we would make it down to the village just in time to watch the light fade beyond the jagged peaks.

That meant there was no hope of returning to the castle today. My thoughts drifted back to the girl who had so curiously wandered into my life from another world, only to be ripped from me in a desperate move made in desperate times. I could only hope that the others were taking care of her in my stead.

Hold on for me, Clara.

4
SABINE

I glanced up from my spellbook, exhausted from a long foray into the ancient magic. Nothing of any real value had been found; these pages were filled with highly experimental spells from an era long gone—from even before the widespread civility that Seven Portals, and its equivalents in the other holds, brought to the greater magical realm. There was no guarantee any of these arcane spells would work.

Just like the spell that the sage found for me...

The lord of the castle sent out summons for a magician. I'd traveled from far across Stonehold, seeing my chance to ingrate myself with the royal family. Lord Elliott Craven was very early in his reign; as far as I was aware, he had no court magician.

It was a horrible oversight.

Chrysm certainly had its uses, but magic was the

supernatural currency used across the world. *The vampire lord really needs to keep a sorcerer of some sort in his employ. Why not me?*

But then my plans took the backstage when I learned *why* he needed access to a powerful caster. *The rumours had been true all along. There really **was** a human on Earth...*

I closed the tome with a weary sigh, glancing down at the unconscious girl. She looked young, like a vampire nearing her first equinox. Were the girl truly one of our kind, her aging would freeze for centuries; she would embody youthful beauty, at least until her aging eventually restarted until she reached the next stage of her life.

But then she'd be powerful.

Such was the case for all of us vampires. The three equinoxes divided us into four eras in our life, in which we embodied a predominant trait.

First, we were young.

Next, we were beautiful.

Then, we were strong.

Finally, we were wise.

But the others watching over her had told me about her strange physiology. Human beings, apparently did not experience equinoxes. From conception, their strange biology marched them right to the grave, living such painfully short and meaningless lives. Whereas the healthiest and most cautious of us could reasonably expect to see a thousand years, the human could at best hope for a tenth of that.

How fascinating, I pondered as I watched her rest. *Their lifetimes are such brief, trembling flickers in the dark. How can you even cope with that? How can you accomplish **anything** of importance when Death plucks you away during a vampire's puberty?*

"You've been buried in that book for days."

I glanced up. One of the three guardians – the friendly, talkative one, at least before his charge dropped into a coma – seemed to have snapped back out of his trance-like rest.

"It's not as hard as you might think," I smiled serenely. "It's called a Focus. It's a trick for steady, prolonged concentration. Especially useful when you need to bury yourself in literature for hours, days, or even longer…"

"You've barely moved an inch," he noted with small admiration. "Not to eat, not to drink… is it really that simple?"

"Sure. Most of my biological functions crawl to a standstill," I replied matter-of-factly. "At face value, it should be similar to that trance skill you possess, since you used to be a royal guard. The difference is that I must extensively recharge my body between uses. It takes a great deal of energy from me to maintain for longer periods of time."

He smirked. "Yeah, ours is way different."

"I'm curious. How does yours work?"

"By the looks of it, you use yours to study." He briefly glanced at the closed tome in my hands. "Ours just shuts our brains off. We become about as useful as your standard statue... but a statue that can spring to life in an instant, ready to defy those who cross us."

"In what way does that serve you?"

"Time's a very boring thing," he replied with a sardonic chuckle. "It wins every battle because it will outlast everything else..."

"Except you?"

"Except us," he agreed. The guardian turned to the nurse on shift; the other was asleep nearby, resting until it was her turn. "Excuse me, but how long has our friend here been winning this little game of 'freeze tag'?"

"Freeze tag?" I asked curiously.

"Yes," the guard smirked. "We teach her of this world. She teaches us of her own. It seems human children like to play strange little games, just as much as *vampire* kids..."

The nurse glanced over with an odd frown. "Clara has been asleep for two days. Closer to three, by now."

"Is that so?" He turned back. "Interesting. It feels more like two *hours* to me. Probably because I keep waking up to walk the perimeter."

"Intriguing," I observed with wonder. "Such a rather

useful skill to have, that. It means that the passage of time means nothing to you. If you were ever trapped somewhere, you and Time itself would be at a stalemate until you were rescued."

"Interesting way of putting it, but yes."

I nodded, stroking the book idly in my arms. *There's something peculiar about him. He feels more powerful than he really is,* I quietly noticed. "I don't believe I ever caught your name."

"Wilhelm," he replied. "You?"

"Sabine."

"Well, Sabine, it's been a fun little chat. I hope you can find way to save our girl in that charming book you've got there. As for me, well, I think it's about time to do another perimeter check..."

"I'll handle it if you'd like. My Focus is getting too hard to maintain, and I must think on things. I'm long overdue for a walk, anyway."

"Do you know the path to take?"

I stood up wearily and walked over to his side. Splaying my fingers across his forehead, I felt out his muscle memory, learning his latest routine for patrolling the area. "I do now."

"You're just full of surprises, aren't you?"

I smirked. "You don't know the half of it."

"Suit yourself, then," Wilhelm shrugged.

With a quick nod to the nurse, I stretched my legs

and walked towards the glass exit. As I gave the room a quick, parting look over my shoulder, I saw that Wilhelm was already back in his trance.

USUALLY, I EXPECTED A CHAPERONE TO SHADOW ME AS I moved around the castle. But these were unusual times. With arguably the most valuable person in the world suspended in a coma, and the master of this kingdom – the vampire lord – whisked away across to the mainland...

The only ruler of this castle right now is chaos.

I knew that Lord Elliott's predecessor was in the castle somewhere, but I hadn't heard even the slightest detail on where. *That's a shame; I wanted to meet the legendary Lorelei Craven sometime.*

Or maybe not, on second thought. *Word is that she's retreated from the public eye for a **reason**...*

Naturally, even without direct supervision, I felt restrictions on my movement. It wasn't as if I had any true intentions to scrutinize the castle to begin with, not beyond wanton curiosity. But we had been locked away in the back of the fortress, in the Craven Keep tower. Servants scurried about in their daily tasks as I wandered the halls, faintly keeping an eye out for any who dared to sneak a look at the unconscious guest.

I had a few suspicions about that spell.

*Well, more accurately about **her**...*

At first, I thought her guardians had grown greatly sloppy in protecting her from the nurses. They barely seemed to pay the other vampires in the room any mind, which made no sense to me. Lord Elliott had made a great fuss over the detail in the old folklore about humans concerning their blood – apparently, just the scent alone was not only highly addictive but utterly intoxicating.

Yet, considering the integrity of their job, the guards didn't show the slightest bit of bother at the other vampires tending to her.

That was my first clue about my suspicions.

Following Lord Elliott's warnings before I'd ever first laid eyes on her, I decided to cast a spell on myself – one specifically designed to dampen hedonistic urges. I'd hoped that it would keep me sane around her blood, if the stories were right about its potency.

It did the trick. I found myself able to manage the way my mouth watered near her.

But my Focus had occupied my time since. Its very nature meant that all other things fell to the wayside, and I'd forgotten to re-energize the spell to keep myself from destroying her. In fact, what little was left of it had been burned up keeping the Focus running, while I studied whatever possibly went wrong in the first place.

Eventually, I drew the conclusion that Clara's guardians must have figured out days ago...

*Albeit, a little haphazardly... the spell **worked**.*

If my suspicions were true, she was safe now. The human could move within the castle without fearing for her life from even the kindest servants in Stonehold Castle. They'd no longer be driven to drain every last drop of blood from Clara's body in an uncontrollable bloodlust.

"You're a curious one."

Snapped from my thoughts, I whirled around to scan the shadows for the sultry, female voice. *I **know** I didn't imagine that...*

My eyes widened. *There.*

Casually perched on an outcropping above, a devious young vampire crunched into an apple. Platinum blond hair flowed over her shoulders as she watched me with the aloof interest of a cat.

"Who might you be?" I asked calmly.

The woman took another crisp bite out of her apple before slipping off from the ledge. With the skill of a gymnast, she effortlessly landed nearby without a broken bone—or a single platinum strand of hair out of place.

"*Surely* my brother has mentioned me..." She purred, rising to a stand. I could see now that the vampire concealed sleek leather armor beneath her cloak; she was dressed as if she spent a great deal of time outside the castle.

"Oh, but of course," I realized with a widening smile. "Nikki Craven, younger sister to the sitting vampire lord. Scourge of the wilds. I've heard stories, but I had no idea you were on the Isle of Obsidian."

Nikki drew closer, a devilish glint in her eyes. *The tales didn't do her justice,* I thought to myself. In those chaotic eyes, I saw a deranged insanity left foolishly unchecked. *She is far more dangerous than I could have ever believed.*

"Stories? Why, I wasn't aware that anybody told stories of little old *me*..." She smiled hungrily. "What kinds of *stories* do the people tell?"

If there could ever be a slinking predator in the shape of another vampire, it was *definitely* this one. "Your sadism is legendary throughout the land," I answered honestly. "When you're sloppy—or when you *want* to, I suspect—you leave quite a lot of destruction in your wake."

"Oh?" Her eyes angrily flared. "Is that so?"

I swallowed. *Not off on the right foot here...*

But then she smiled sweetly. "You flatter me."

"I only speak what I hear, my Lady." I let out a breath of relief. She was truly as unpredictable as they said; in less than two minutes alone with her, I couldn't tell if her mental state made her more likely to attack or compliment me.

This one is a wildcard, I decided. *If I really **had** to, I know that I could destroy her. But I'd rather just slip away and stay in her good graces...*

Nikki's pleased grin evaporated in an instant. "I know why you are here, Sabine. And it's not just because of the human, is it?"

I froze. "What?"

Lord Elliott's sister grinned sadistically as she studied my expression. "You barely know me, my darling sorceress, but believe me... I have spent a long time out in the greater hold. I know its secrets." She drew even closer now; her eyes widened darkly. "And I know *yours...*"

I quickly grasped my mistake in letting this one so close. *Nikki clearly thinks she is talking to someone else; that's the only explanation that makes any logical sense—*

"You want to become a vassal."

I blinked in surprise. "A what?"

"Don't lie to me, Sabine." Her voice took on an affectionate tone again. "Our mother dispensed of the vassal system, early in her reign. But if Elliott brings it back and makes you one, you'll become a permanent member of this castle—and have constant access to the vampire lord. That means no more hiding out in the abandoned graveyards of Sifter's Hollow like a rat... "

I was stunned. "I was the town sorceress! I—"

"Oh, don't pretend. We *both* know you were no more an official magician than *I* a productive, mentally stable member of society," she narrowed her eyes. *Oh good,* I groaned. *So this one's well aware that she's madder than a hatter. But is that better—or **worse?*** "You did what you had to do to survive. I know the sacrifices you had to make, both in your best interests and in others... you single-handedly kept the black revenants from rising and slaughtering Sifter's Hollow, and they rewarded you with *fear*. They *reviled* you. So you hid along the edges of the town, doing what you had to in order to *endure*..."

How? I snarled in my head. *How does she know so much about me? There isn't a vampire outside the village who should know **anything** about those risen monstrosities...*

"So, given the *high esteem* they rewarded you, calling yourself 'the Sorceress of Sifter's Hollow' is quite a stretch of the imagination..."

This had gone on long enough; I began to fear whatever else she might know if she kept talking. "Lady Craven, what is it that you want?"

"A partnership," she cooed.

"What are you talking about?"

"You have a plan," she smiled wickedly. "This little *hiccup* with the human means that you have to improvise more than you thought, but I know you have something in mind... and I want in."

I studied her eyes. Nikki Craven was perfectly

unreadable, and that made her dangerous. *But it could make her an interesting ally, and it seems she's already got me partly figured out...*

*But not **entirely**,* I decided with a smirk.

"Let's say you're right. Let's pretend that I've come to the castle with more *ambitious* motives. Let's pretend I want to be more than just a caster, blown in off the distant winds. What could you stand possibly to gain?"

Her eyes lit up, like those of a stalking hunter. "War is coming, and I aim to build a stacked deck. My dearest Elliott hasn't seen the value in having a powerful friend in an unsanctioned sorceress... let's just say I think a little more outside the box."

So the rumours are already spreading across the hold, then. I should alert my allies abroad at once. I wonder, ever so curiously, what my old highborn friend will think of all these strange developments...

"And what would be the nature of this...?"

"Partnership?" She helpfully finished.

"Yes," I nodded. "This *partnership...*"

For once, Nikki seemed suddenly aware of our surroundings. "A discussion for a time of privacy, I think." Her devilish eyes trained onto mine as she held out a hand. "Do we have a deal?"

*This deranged vampire is clearly dangerous... but she is **nothing** in comparison to the trials I have endured. They may have ultimately denied sanctioning me at the academy—but I'm* *still one of the most powerful unregistered magicians in the entire hold, possibly the world. I've built a network of powerful friends across some of the other holds. With even the slightest preparation, I can punish her if she **dares** to cross me...*

But something shook me down to my core.

*She speaks of war, coming across the holds... Nikki Craven must **know** something. And whatever it is, I can't very well ascend rank without knowing what it is...*

I shook her hand.

"Lady Craven, I believe we have a deal."

5

ELLIOTT

As I'd suspected, the setting sun only lingered in the peaks long enough to watch us climb out from our improvised transport.

My gaze took in the village as my boots hit the dirt. Most of these buildings were the bunkhouses for the mining force, but others sat stocked with the afterhours services offered to the workers.

Of this small village, almost everyone toiled in the Dawning Mines. But they worked schedules that kept them here for years at a time; half the small town above was stocked with vampires and amenities to keep the workers happy, all of who were glad to have consistent customers.

The gambling hall was, naturally, the largest and most obvious building. But there were other ways to be entertained here; at a glance, I spotted restaurants, shops, and tradesmen in their huts. Two bars even competed for the nightly attention of the workforce. Combined, it all took what could have been a few downcast bunkhouses outside an unforgiving mine, and built them into a thriving and vibrant nighttime village.

Strong walls of log kept out the local wildlife, reinforced by a local spell-caster. With all the free magic in our world, creatures from beyond our wildest imaginations lurked in the darkest places. The miners needed constant protection, and there were some things out here that even a strong wall wouldn't stop.

"Home, sweet home," Pavric chuckled after he saw how I took in my environment. "Well, at least hopefully it *stays* that way..."

"What's that?" I turned.

"Oh. Better for *them* to explain."

The welcoming party greeted us as the guards took their positions at my side. Several old miners and their apprentices wiped themselves clean and stepped forward to bow.

One elderly vampire in particular appeared to be in charge here. Old, raggedy, and afflicted with quite the unforgettable moustache, he stepped forward to greet me. "Lord Craven! Allow me to welcome you to the Dawning Mines. Did you enjoy the ride down the mountains?"

"Indeed. I apparently picked the right time of day to come. The views are spectacular."

He grinned pleasantly. "Good day for it, too. Been raining something fierce the past few weeks. You'd have been disappointed."

"You should learn that I'm *never* disappointed when things get accomplished," I warned him irritably. "Which, incidentally enough, brings me to why I am here..."

"Straight to the point, huh? Your mother was always like that, too." The miner replied wryly before turning to the others. "You heard the man. Assemble the guild in the meeting hall..."

I confidently followed them inside with my guards at the flank, utterly unprepared for what I was about to hear. What was happening here in the Dawning Mines cast a much larger shadow than any mere worker's strike...

PAVRIC AND THE ELDER STOOD STEADFAST TO THE SIDE as the hall filled with the mining crew.

They looked exhausted and frightened.

That **can't** *be simply because I'm here,* I silently reasoned. *What could be going on here, then, that terrifies grizzled workers as strong as these ones?*

The Elder waved towards me, long before the workforce had fully amassed. *The others must be in the mines still. Good. Let them continue the work while I get to the bottom of this...*

"It is my pleasure to introduce Elliott Craven, vampire lord of Stonehold! He's come from across the sea to listen to our concerns."

A voice rang out from among them.

"Took him bloody well long enough!"

"Who said that?" The Elder fiercely snapped. "Was it you, Cadic? I'll have your throat! How *dare* you speak that way in front of your lord!"

Slipping myself into a furious calm, I tried to wait out the disruption with eyes closed and my arms crossed. When it was clear that nothing of the sort was happening, I stomped a boot to the floor and snapped alert for them.

"Silence! *All of you!*"

The guild didn't dare to test me, and the room fell into a stunned quiet. The royal guards at my back fanned defensively around me, but I paid no heed to them.

With a sympathizing voice that relinquished none of my anger, I defiantly conceded the point. "You're right. I have taken far too long to come here, and you all have my apologies. But know that I would not ignore this... not unless there was *something else* taking my attention."

I sighed, relaxing my posture.

"But you have it now."

The guildhall stood silent. For all the worries and fretting of my high chancellor, these workers all of a sudden seemed very reluctant to speak, now that I had crossed the distance between their humble village and my personal throne room.

Someone asked: "Lord Craven, is it true?"

I narrowed my eyes. "Is *what* true?"

"That there's a human in your castle."

The entire assembly broke into murmurs, and I groaned. Every eye in the place was on me; I slid my hardened gaze across the packed chamber.

"Yes," I finally responded. "A human is here."

Murmurs rose from the crowd. It was not the first time I'd needed to embrace this conversation, and it definitely wouldn't be the last. I couldn't help but be annoyed, wondering to myself: *how many more times are enough?*

But I saw an opening, and continued. "There is a human girl in Stonehold Castle. She is in grave danger, and I must attend to her shortly. I left her side to come here, to speak to all of you."

That got their attention.

"So, when I have such delicate matters on my mind, you might understand my vast annoyance at being called here over a worker's strike, more so when *none of you* seem willing to—"

"My Lord, you have it wrong."

I turned to confront the voice; it was Pavric.

"Then explain it to me—because my patience is being continuously tested." My arms folded over my chest. "The high chancellor tells me that our chrysm production dwindles. He tells me that none of you will allow outsiders anywhere *near* the Dawning Mines." With mounting anger, I slightly tilted my head. "So, somebody please enlighten me... what the *hell* is going on out here?"

The others remained silent. Pavric looked like he regretted drawing my attention, and for damn good reason.

"There is a beast," the elder spoke up.

"A beast?" I arched an eyebrow.

"Yes, my Lord. Something terrible haunts us. It has appeared in the mines, slaughtering some of our finest workers from the thickest shadows. The darkness below conceals the creature, and it comes for us when we dig."

"You have magical barriers in place."

"For the outside, yes. But the beast came from *inside* the mountains. It came during a routine excavation... it was already here in the mines."

I was intrigued. "Tell me more."

The elder solemnly averted his troubled gaze. "None of us have seen it and lived, Lord Craven. We can only hear the hideous noises, both when it hunts and when it... eats."

I tilted my head. *It's not unheard of for an apex predator to appear in the untamed wilds, but... from beneath the ground?*

"How long has it been here?"

"A few weeks," Pavric explained. "At first, we didn't realize it was anything out of the ordinary. The creature slowly began picking us off, never more than one of us at a time. But success seems to have made the beast bolder. It strikes far more often now, without mercy or warning. We cannot mine for more than a few hours, day or night, before it comes for us."

"How many have died?"

The elder sighed. "This is all who are left."

I glanced around the room in total disbelief. "The Dawning Mines are the largest subterranean operation in the entire hold... possibly the world. There should be just shy of a hundred vampires on these premises alone!" I closed the distance to the elder, looking him dead in the eyes. "Are you telling me that this creature has taken over *half* of your people?"

He blinked his gaze away. "Yes."

My disbelief evaporated, leaving only stunned silence in its wake. I walked away and put a palm against a support beam. "Fifty vampires... dead?"

"More," he sullenly clarified. "Sadly, my Lord, we can never reclaim the bodies to confirm. It's likely at least several of the missing miners are deserters, seeing their opportunity to escape the work. But for the most part,

I'm of the inclination that the rampant beast has killed possibly sixty or seventy vampires altogether."

"That's unprecedented," I muttered.

"It is. It's also a tragedy and a disaster. We just can't safely continue operations with something like that lurking in the dark."

"No," I agreed. "Nor could I expect you to. But the world has grown reliant on the vast chrysm stores buried in these mines. The harvest cannot be allowed to stop."

"Of course not," the elder replied. "But Lord Craven, what would you have us do? It thins our numbers ever more by the day. It's only a matter of time before it comes for the village. After another two weeks of this, I fear there will be nobody down here to *mine* these caverns for you."

"Simple. Fetch me the best weapons you have, and prepare to make up for the production losses. In the meantime, I need every available detail you have on this creature."

"You intend to drive it away?"

"If what you're telling me is true, then this insolent beast has killed half the workforce on my chrysm mines. There *is* no 'driving it away.' It's tasted blood and developed a lust for massacre." Filled with wrathful ferocity, I vehemently stared down the elder guildsman. "It's in the wrong place at the wrong time. This creature threatens to upset the world's balance in ways anarchists could only *dream* of. Given the danger, there's only one proper choice left before me…"

"And what is that, my Lord?"

I could feel my expression darkening. *Clara would **hate** the idea, but she's under the best care my realm can provide —and while she sleeps, I have a hold to rule…* "I must descend below the surface and destroy the beast, *myself.*"

6

ELLIOTT

Beneath the earth, day and night meant nothing.

My guards came armed for combat, but there was a difference between fighting other vampires and fending off a vicious magical creature—let alone, an apex predator.

Maybe I should have brought Nikki after all. I've heard a few of the stories of how she's kept herself occupied, all these years... But it was too late to head back to the castle now.

Luckily, the miners were proactive enough to start stockpiling any available combat gear once they confirmed the beast's presence. There was no telling what I'd face down below, but one look at their sword selection told me that the mystery creature held all the advantages.

But beggars can't be choosers; the weapons on hand were still more fitted to the task than what my guards had arrived with in camp. I wasted no time in securing them better weaponry. With my approval, they checked the weights and dexterity of various axes, swords, and spears before settling on whatever felt most comfortable.

Meanwhile, I suited myself in the best-fitting armor the miners could dig up for me. I'd arrived without a weapon; from their disappointing load, considering the close quarters of possibly fighting in a mine, I chose a bladed quarterstaff. *An odd choice, I'll admit—but the one I'm best-trained with. It'll allow me to drive the thing back into the depths, at the very least—and let my guards finish it off...*

Pavric and the elder greeted us as we left the improvised barracks in the back of the village. In the intervening time, the sun was but a memory. Darkness had long since descended, and the stars were out to paint the sky in their twinkling glory.

"My Lord, are you certain it's wise to go now?" The elder spoke in a hushed tone. "Why not take the night and send for reinforcements?"

"You said it yourself: the creature could come out from the mines at any moment. After all these centuries of continuous mining, it certainly didn't live there before." I gave Pavric an appraising look as we walked towards the digging transport. "What else do you know of the beast?"

"The elder could tell you more," he noted with a glum

look. "Personally, I've no experience with the creature myself."

I paused. "You told me you're a master miner. I was under the impression that you had to work in the mines with the others to hold the title."

The elder barked loudly. "Hah! Did he now?" He cut me a dour glance. "The title was inherited."

"*Inherited?*" My eyes narrowed on Pavric. "Do not make a mockery of tradition in my presence. How many years did you spend working below, in the mines?"

My guide was sheepish. "Lord Craven, my role was always a lot more... administrative."

I scoffed. "Typical. Just typical."

I turned to the elder. "Fine. If you know more, then tell me more. How do I lure the beast? What do I need to do to face it?"

"It responds to vampires," he observed coolly. "It never takes more than a few hours to attack when it senses one, so baiting isn't necessary."

"I don't expect to wait very long, then."

"Why's that?"

"My physiology. A vampire lord is much more than an *inherited* title," I cast a meaningful glance in Pavric's direction, and he cowered. "My blood is more magically attuned than standard vampires. If the creature senses through magical intuition, as many of the larger ones do, then my presence should be a beacon in the dark."

The elder merely nodded. "I suppose I'm not terribly surprised, then. Perhaps it is best for you to descend tonight after all. If you stayed in the village until dawn, you might draw the creature out to slaughter half the village in their sleep."

"Precisely what I was thinking."

Pavric visibly paled.

PUTTERING WITH SMOKY EXHAUST OUT THE TOP VENTS, the freight elevator groaned as it slowly lowered my troop into the mines.

"Lord Craven, why not use the digger?" Pavric was the only miner's guild member to volunteer for the mission, apparently in a bid to curry favour with the rest. It made sense in the revelation of his *true* duties here—I imagined banking on his ancestor's glory was not terribly popular with the others. The look on his face, however, betrayed that he'd come to regret taking the opportunity. "We could have driven down there in safety with a quick exit…"

My eyes narrowed. "How often is that piece of equipment used in operations?"

"It's the first thing we send out."

"That's why," I replied coolly. "Not only does the machine rob me of the element of surprise, but the beast can hear that machine's footprint from half an hour out. My hope is that introducing my presence to the equation puts the creature on the wrong foot. Maybe it's gotten sloppy, and we might get the jump on it. Besides..."

Taking a step forward, I scrutinized our ride down. Compared to this ramshackle husk, I was the epitome of youth. With little more than a ceiling and a floor, the elevator was a shuddering, metallic skeleton of a thing, and came from a time long before widespread chrysm use.

"My Lord?"

I snapped back to reality and turned to Pavric. "I do not believe that it came here naturally. The beast, whatever it is, has encroached on our mines. *It* is the intruder, not us. I refuse to face it at the entrance like a sniveling, begging child – no, I will face it in the heart of its lair."

For a moment, I saw something flash across his eyes. It was either respect or mockery.

"You're nothing like what I thought you'd be, Lord Craven. I think I disagree with the elder. You make quite a different vampire lord from the one who came before."

"Power casts a strong shadow," I explained. "As time passes, that power interweaves with those who wield it. They become inseparable, and their shadows become one. But power can never truly last. When the time comes for it to change hands, all else is meaningless until the new steps out from the shadow of the old. Lorelei

Craven became a powerful ruler and spearheaded a new age for our world—in time, perhaps so can I..."

Pavric was curiously thoughtful.

"That's what you intend to do?"

The elevator lurched to a stop; the basic rails groaned apart, and the shining mine of glowing, blood red chrysm ore awaited us.

I turned to him, leaning against my weapon. It was at least two heads taller than I was. "Pavric, of all the varied weapons your guild stocked, why do you think I chose a quarterstaff?"

He frowned, shaking his head. "I imagine you have a lot of training with it, or something close."

My fist slid a grip further up the quarterstaff, and I admired the subtle curve of the point atop it: a tapered, sharpened blade. "You're right, I do. But there's more to it than that. Without more to know about our feral enemy down below, I picked a proud and maneuverable weapon. In constraint, it's not an efficient tool. But used wisely..."

Stepping forward from the elevator, I held a hand out to order my guards back. "It can parry." I took a defensive stance, holding it in both hands. "It can redirect." I pretended to knock back a blow. "It can strike, and it can defend." I mimicked the other moves and began to twirl it all around with expertise afforded by decades of trained intimacy. All the while, my hands danced along the weapon, shifting it from both hands, to one, to plucking it from the air in a restrained somersault. "This pole allows me to control all the space around me. It shifts easily from hand to hand. In a second, with the slightest shift of my control, it becomes whatever I need it to be. In such a basic weapon," I leapt in vaulted kicks, whipping the quarterstaff around and effortlessly switching between hands, "I've found the weapon with which I identify most."

"Impressive," he nodded with a stunned look on his face. "I think I get it."

"You don't." I spun it with my palm above, butting it hard against the ground at my boots. "Highly versatile, inherently adaptable, and truly unbending... in both my reign and my own mind, this tool represents everything I aim to ever be."

"You've forgotten one," Pavric observed.

"Oh?" My head tilted. "What's that?"

"A powerful and very capable tool, sure, only when placed in the right hands." Cheerily smiling, he stepped out from the elevator with the rest of my guards. "This weapon you've chosen is an odd one, I'll admit, but after such a demonstration..."

He pulled closer. My guards cautiously placed a hand to their weapons, and he stopped. "I stand by what I said earlier, Lord Craven. You'll make a far different ruler than your mother ever was. That much is already obvious. But what I wonder is, after this talk of weapons and tools…"

The guildsman aloofly smiled. "What kind of tool will the world make *you*, my Lord?"

Beneath the earth, the deposits of exposed chrysm ore bathed the mineshafts in a hellish glow.

The royal guards were flanked out around me as we marched forwards, weapons at the ready. None of them would admit it, but I didn't need any supernatural help to sense the apprehension. *Nothing else has quite the demoralizing effect of 'Tonight, march with me into Hell…'*

But these were loyal men and women, serving at my side. Any one of them would die for me.

Let's hope it doesn't come to that.

There was only one other sound in the mines: the infernal, trickling dripping of a nearby river. We could hear the water on the other side of the cavern wall, as if it were mocking us.

I brushed past the young, capable guard in front. Much like Asarra—the youngest guard in the castle, but one who was chosen to help protect Clara Blackwell—this one was also a comparably young female warrior. *Kinsey*, I recalled her name. *A veteran not in age but skill—a true prodigy of the blade…*

"My Lord?"

"No," I told her sternly. "I'll take point. Ensure that the creature doesn't flank us. When it sees us, it will come for me. Take your chance to bring the beast down while it's distracted."

The guard obeyed, sliding into rear formation behind me and taking a defensive stance.

With the trickling water aiming to gradually unnerve the group, the six of us continued deeper into the heart of the Dawning Mines. The chrysm was so plentiful down here that the miners hadn't bothered arranging for alternate lighting; it must have felt to them like they were digging their way deeper and deeper into Hell.

No wonder they're growing superstitious. With centuries in an atmosphere like this, my mind would start to drift into madness as well...

"Did you hear that, my Lord?"

"No." I froze mid-step.

A distant scraping noise hit my ears.

"There," a guard noted. "There it is again."

I turned to my entourage, scanning their eyes for signs of weakness. The shaft was carved wide enough for us to walk shoulder-to-shoulder, but it was little consolation. *Ever since the first stumbling steps of our society, vampires have lived outside the bleak, rudimentary caves of old...*

Unsurprisingly, they were terrified. I couldn't bring myself to march them another step further if they didn't have it in them. "I'll give all of you this one opportunity to turn back," I warned the others. "There's no disgrace in it. But to those who choose to stay, I need complete confidence in your courage and bravery, because my life will be held in your hands..."

The guards steeled themselves; none of them turned from my eyes.

"Good. Then let us find and destroy this—"

A shrieking growl, vicious enough to tremble the hearts of fearless men, roared throughout the mineshaft. The others shivered at its intensity as we turned around.

A guard gasped. "That came from back there."

"That's where the exit is!"

I held them back with a hand! "Silence. Let me listen, all of you..." But all that I could hear was the damned trickling of water behind the cavern walls. It mocked me harder than ever, daring to distract me in this moment of life and death.

"Whatever it is," I snarled, "it's bigger than we were led to believe. There's no way something like that can move undetected in this place..."

Another low growl rumbled out.

"It's closer!" A guard blurted in terror.

"Yes," I narrowed my eyes. "*Too* close..." With a quick glance over my shoulder, I spat the order: "Arms at the ready, all of you!" I turned back to face the way we'd approached. "It's coming..."

At least we had a strategic advantage.

"Listen, all of you. We still have the upper hand. We lost the element of surprise, but it can only face one or two of us at a time. It'll be too constrained in here to attack us all at once..."

"That's right," someone murmured.

"Come!" I rallied the troops. "Whatever it is, the hell-beast stands between us and our way out. I want us back on that elevator, *all of us,* with the head of this creature. Lift your swords, my sworn guards, and *follow your lord into battle!*"

They belted in unison: "Hoo-rah!"

With my quarterstaff held confidently and a handful of guards at my flank, I ran back the way we'd come towards our exit. *Whatever you are, you monstrosity, the sun will rise over your corpse...*

We turned a corner and gazed into the furious eyes of Death itself. As the huge creature whipped towards us, I heard the terrified gasps ring out at my back and I knew, in a heartbeat, the truth of our situation. My bolting strides slowed to a stop. Suddenly, the quarterstaff felt heavy in my hands, because I *recognized* this damned monstrosity. I knew what our chances of survival, even *mine*, were...

One thought drowned out all others.

I've killed us all.

7

CLARA

When I woke up, the light was overwhelming.

Oblique images flashed through my mind – stray fragments from my dreams. But it was hard to focus on them in my overwhelming pain. The brightness above shone so blindingly strong; it even partly breached my closed eyelids. Lethargic and deeply disoriented, I sluggishly tried to shield my eyes. But I found that I couldn't lift my arms. The limbs felt rebelliously heavy, and they would only barely move at my urging.

Worse still, my scratchy throat was intensely dry. I urgently needed water. Just trying to utter a syllable hurt. There was barely any moisture left in my mouth. My parched tongue had swollen into a thick, heavy mass that wouldn't obey my orders. On top of it all, my throbbing, pounding headache liquefied what little brainpower I could muster into unintelligible mush.

I tried to focus on the few available details.

Apparently, I was on my back in some kind of bed. There were people nearby, but they weren't talking. I couldn't reach them, but at least I wasn't left alone here – wherever 'here' turned out to be. *Everything hurts,* I moaned in my head. *If I could just somehow tell them to make it stop...*

I felt trapped in my own body.

Annoyance morphed into desperation. Driven by a frantic need to retreat from the light, I threw everything I had into at least turning away from the pain.

A shoulder twitched.

Come on come on **come on COME ON***...*

If I could've grit my teeth, I'd have probably ground them all into dust. It was getting harder to breathe; I felt my lungs seizing as I clenched my body tight, trying to force myself to roll over. In a distant sort of way, I noticed a beeping.

"What's that incessant noise?"

I recognized that voice.

Asarra...

"No idea!" That was one I didn't know. I felt a presence suddenly near me; something like fabric brushed against my arm for a fleeting second. "It looks like the machine's malfunctioning again. Typical! Why is Lord

Craven even insisting that we bother with this old thing?"

"Is there any way to make that stop?" *Viktor,* I realized with a sense of relief. *If the two of* them *are here, then that means...*

Wilhelm's voice chimed in. "Maybe we should just leave it alone." He spoke mirthlessly. "The bloody thing's loud enough to wake the dead. We've tried damn well near everything else to save the poor girl. Maybe all that infernal beeping will get her up."

I felt the fabric brush against my arm again as the strange woman shifted in place. *Alrighty then, Clara. New plan...*

Instead of forcing myself to roll over, I tried to drag my wrist closer to her clothing. *Come on, hand. I've never asked much of you, have I? Just be a doll and do me this one solid...*

The wrist wouldn't budge.

But the *elbow* would.

I could barely feel my teeth touch as I tried to grit them again. Forcing my elbow to pivot at the approximate speed of drying paint, I screamed in my head with anxious fervor. Gradually, the side of my hand dragged along the duvet with barely noticeable progress...

The beeping stopped.

"There!" The stranger spoke up.

To my horror, I realized that my window was closing.

I could only scarcely tell where my arms were in relation to my body, and the light was so blindingly bright in my eyes that I feared it would take my sight forever.

*If I don't die of dehydration first... but, my god, how am I **this** dehydrated? What have these people been **doing** to me?*

She walked around the bed, brushing my arm again. This time, my splayed fingers were just on the edge of the bedding and close enough to touch her clothing...

I seized the opportunity. With my final ounce of strength, I twitched my fingertips and snagged the tightest grip on the soft fabric that I could. She didn't notice, and she didn't stop – which was just like I wanted it.

Please, please, PLEASE be enough, I begged.

My clenched grip caught, and she accidentally yanked me halfway out the bed.

"What on earth?" She gasped.

I had misjudged. In my desperation, were it not for a split second of lightning-fast intervention, I would have cracked my skull against the floor.

But someone had caught me.

The commotion had jarred open my dry eyes. If I could have screamed in pain, I would have. But Asarra's confused face filled my vision as she held me cradled against her. The machine was beeping like never before, and my hearing slowly adjusted to take it in. It was intensely loud.

"What in the *hell* just happened?" She angrily blurted, looking over at someone else. "How did you rip her out of her bed?"

"Hey, I have no idea!" The stranger protested. "I think her hand hooked my robe!"

Asarra started to lift me back into the bed, her Slavic accent brimming irritably. "You *must* be more careful than that. Lord Elliott has made it clear what might happen if Clara drops dead on our watch..."

No, stop! I screamed in my head, desperately trying to shift my pupils around. *Look at me! Why can't you see that I'm awake?!*

"I'm *very* aware of Master Craven's demands," the voice petulantly replied. "And quite frankly, I don't need such foolish reminders. We've been at this for days! Don't you think we could use a little less stress?"

Asarra shook her head angrily, averting her gaze to me in her arms. "Count yourself *very* lucky that I..." Her eyes caught my stare, and she tilted her head in slight curiosity. Her face loomed just a little closer. "What the...?"

Trapped in my silence, I watched her eyes slowly widen in dawning comprehension.

"Gods alive! *Clara?!*"

Suddenly, half a dozen faces were behind her and staring into mine. I recognized the rest of the Knightly Trio, and then there was that sorceress, Nikki was here...

and, well, those other two I didn't know. They looked like they were possibly nurses, maybe. But everyone's expressions ran the gamut from plain terror to complete relief.

Thinking quickly—and this is why I love this girl—she lowered her ear to my dried, chapped lips. "If you can say *anything*, little Clara..."

"Water," I barely squeaked. "Too bright. *Please...*"

Asarra nodded and glanced up from cradling me. "You there, kill the lights – and for gods' sakes, someone get this girl some water!"

8
ELLIOTT

Bearing down on us, the serpentine beast roared with a furry head shaped as a seven-pointed star. Long ears tapered off into what looked like horns; below them, two thick clumps of hair jutted in large tufts out behind either cheek, framing a matted beard that dragged near the ground; a pair of vicious, primitive saber-teeth jutted down from its snarling jowls.

The chilling combination made a terrifying sight – it was almost enough to distract from the pair of thick, furry, coiled arms, both of which ended in razor-sharp paws the size of my chest.

The entire front of the creature was a horrific, magical twist on a feral lynx. The orangish-brown fur that coated the monstrosity gave way to four long meters of snake, ending in a sinister rattle. The fur extended down a third of the snakeskin's back, serving as a thick mohawk from where sharp protrusions rose out of its back.

But the worst part was its eyes. The monster came at us with sinister, glowing yellow eyes. The feline pupils only highlighted the viciousness of the abomination as it hunted.

I know what you are, I glowered at the beast. *Sure, I'll probably die this day, but at least I won't be slain with complete ignorance of my murderer's **true** nature...*

Summoning whatever strength of character I could, I turned my terror into fury. Whipping my quarterstaff into the air, I spun it for momentum and thrust the blade into the monster's face.

Dodging backwards, it rattled its tail with a malicious snarl. But the opening gave my guards the chance to match my courage with their own.

Five armed, experienced warriors lunged past me with every weapon drawn at the ready. They landed in a fanned position in front; without giving it a moment's peace, they launched a unified assault against the whipping, snarling abomination before us.

The name of the game was no longer 'slay the beast.' Now, all that concerned me was *get the hell out of here*.

Unfortunately it perched between us and our one way out. There was no option of a tactical retreat; the best we could hope for was simply driving it back until it fled further into the mines.

But the monster was a daredevil, and it was a rather intelligent one. With the natural hunting instincts of a preying cat and the wicked cunning of a slithering snake, the magical beast began to test the stalwart formation of my royal guards. It lunged towards us with gnashing jaws that could crush armor, and swiped our way with a vast paw strong enough to shatter ribs.

One particular guard couldn't dodge in time. Bashed straight into the rocky side of the hallway, he crumpled to the floor in a complete daze.

The others took the brief distraction and tried to launch a counter-attack. But the beast was able to repel them, powerfully dodging and whipping around in the constrained space.

That's when I dove forward.

The guards struck in trained unison, forcing the creature backwards; with my quarterstaff up, I lunged past their formation and leapt over its paw, slicing at the creature's face. It roared in pain and swiped powerfully – I couldn't avoid the impact in mid-air, and it knocked the wind out of my lungs.

I was sent barreling to the ground, only able to land dexterously at the last instant. The others jumped over me and attacked again; I struggled to regain my complete vision.

Screams tore through my disorientation. One of my guards lay dead on the ground – his armor was a mangled mess, punctured by a mighty slash of the paw. The others fought demoralization and clashed against it simply to protect me. With a glance, I checked on the other downed guard – still slumped beside the wall and clearly not moving anytime soon.

I have to save them, I groaned in my head.

*If I could just get **closer**...*

My stray hand reached for the quarterstaff, and regret dawned on me as I felt it in my grasp. I'd been downright foolish to rush attacking this beast; the same applied to picking this weapon. *There's no way I can use this properly with others in the fighting area. I should have realized this tool is just too unwieldy with allies nearby...*

My eyes caught those of the beast. On a whim, it lunged for me – before I could raise my weapon, another guard intervened. The wound was fatal. In the chaos, her body crashed into mine, and we clattered down together.

As I smashed my head against the ground, I blacked out to the sounds of a losing battle...

※

WHEN I AWOKE, THE SMELL OF DEATH ENVELOPED ME.

Only the sound of trickling water greeted me. Realizing that the monster was gone, I started to groggily push the heavy body of a guard off of me.

My trembling fingers touched the caked blood on my

forehead as I climbed to my feet. Wearily, I steadied myself with a palm against the wall and gazed around the chrysm mine, trying to make sense of it all despite my head trauma. What I saw stole the very breath from my lungs.

All five of my guards were dead.

No, I gasped. *This can't be happening...*

I dropped to my knees near, the female guard who had swapped ranks with me in formation. Her helmet was scattered to the side, dented in—and her flowing, dark red hair was matted with filth and dust against the ground. Shivering in regret, my hands reached out to her hair and stroked it.

I'd taken it upon myself to know the names of all my guards, many years before I was ever granted the throne and made to undergo the Ascension. As for this one—a faithful servant forever asleep at my knees... *I was **just** thinking of your prodigal talent, Kinsey...*

"I'm... I'm so sorry," I whispered as I wiped her forehead clean and planted a peck against it. "This didn't have to happen. You saved my life. Please, I have no right to ask, but... forgive me."

Her lifeless eyes offered neither judgment nor compassion. I closed them with my fingertips. My head bowed as everything inside filled with a great and powerful grief.

If only I'd know, I howled in my head. *None of us stood a chance against that thing. They didn't tell Silas anything about a magical beast! I'd have come here with a bloody battalion of guards to kill it!*

My shoulders collapsed.

"No," I whispered. "The fault is my own. I'm just as much to blame. I led these servants into danger, and they paid the ultimate price..."

My gaze lifted, and I stared down the hallway.

I will not let their sacrifice be in vain, and I will not let them rot in this place...

When I moved to lift her, she coughed – and I almost jumped out of my own skin. Dropping back to her side on my knees, I checked her wounds while she seemingly stirred back to life.

She wasn't the only one. The others started to murmur, save the one I watched die.

"I watched that thing slaughter *half* of you," I muttered in disbelief. "After what we've just been through, how are *any* of you still alive?"

The guard winced. I took her hand, pulled her to a sitting position, and helped her put her back to the wall. "I don't know," she groaned in pain. "I think I lost a lot of blood, but I only faded out. The beast didn't kill me..."

Shock, I thought. *I must have just been in shock. Unless the beast drips with stunning poison—a very rare trait with **those** particular things...*

I took her head in both hands and, filled with the

harrowing things we'd seen, pressed my forehead to hers. "I will never lead any of you into death like that again."

She laughed and winced. "Lord Elliott, we all live to serve. Lead us wherever you need to, but... maybe next time, we could head back to the castle for reinforcements?"

A weary chuckle left my lungs. "Deal."

I glanced over my shoulder at the others. Still, only one appeared to actually be dead – the others were waking back up from the horrific aftermath. "If you're okay for the moment, I need to check on the others..."

"Do what you must, my Lord."

Leaving her side, I took stock of the guards. It seemed they were all badly hurt, even hovering at the edge of death, but with medical attention they would all make it... minus the one.

I glanced haggardly at the one in torn, bleeding armour against the ground. *No magic alive, I fear, will do anything for **that** one... but your sacrifice will not be in vain.*

Dedicated to getting everyone else out of harm's way as fast as possible, I scooped up two vampires over my shoulders and wearily carried them back to the elevator. To my complete dismay, our ride back up was gone. I had to sit the wounded guards down near the base and use the winch to recall it from far above on the surface.

While I waited on that, I returned to scoop up another two guards. This time, I grabbed the dead one as well – I was determined to ensure that he at least received a proper burial for his selfless sacrifice.

The elevator still hadn't finished lowering as I approached, so I slumped them down together to return for the final guard. She barely spoke out of pain and misery, so I gingerly carried her over my shoulder with the quarterstaff retrieved and held in my dominant fist. *No telling when that creature will rear its ugly head again... can't hurt for me to be at least **partly** prepared...*

I navigated the tunnel without issue. When I finally made it back to the lower bay, the elevator had arrived at last. As carefully as I could, I began moving my wounded guards into the elevator to send them back up to Gransome Village.

"Lord Elliott," Kinsey grunted painfully. "We can still kill this thing. I just need a bit more time to heal up. I think we can put it out of our misery after we've rejuvenated..."

"Not fast enough," I insisted gravely. "Maybe. But you are in no condition to fight anymore. The best thing you can do right now is–"

I froze when I heard the growling again.

"Oh *gods*," she groaned in horror. "That *thing* is coming back again–"

Without a moment to lose, I moved the rest of them into the elevator and began preparing it for ascent again.

Kinsey must have seen the defeated look on my face; she reached for me in a coughing fit. "Wait," she choked on the word. "Lord Elliott—you're going to come up with us, aren't you? We can live to fight that thing another day..."

I looked up from the control panel. "That *thing* has a name—and if we'd only known it before, this would have never happened. When you return to the surface... tell them all that a full-grown Tatzelwurm has appeared in the Dawning Mines."

"Gods," she paled. "*That's* what that was? I've heard stories, but I thought the infernal creatures were *extinct*..."

I nodded gravely. "We never stood a chance."

One of the greatest mythological perils of Stonehold —tatzelwurms were nightmares given flesh and blood. Not once in my life had I thought I'd *ever* see one, let alone face one in combat. News of them was few and far between, as they lived far up in the mountains and never came down to the main roads or settlements. Vampires typically had too little flesh on their bones for *those* hellish beasts... no, these abominations feasted on the *other* nightmares of the surrounding chaotic wilds. *It's really no **wonder** the people think they're extinct—or mere tales.*

The lights in the elevator switched back on. It was just in time for the serpentine monstrosity to slither back into view; I tightened my grip on the quarterstaff as it lunged for the elevator.

"No!" I snapped the blade at it, driving it back. My furious eyes vehemently stared into the beast. "So long as I draw breath, you will *not* take them!"

"Lord Elliott!" The guard pleaded. "Lord Elli–"

The switch flipped – the rails snapped shut. The elevator groaned to life and steadily started rising as Kinsey slowly pulled herself towards me. "No!" She reached down through the rails. "Lord Elliott, take my hand!"

"Don't be stupid," I grunted wearily as I swept the quarterstaff into a defensive stance. "The cave will rip your arm off if you hold it out like that. Go back to the surface... I'll hold it here for now."

The tatzelwurm loomed closer. Malevolently, its attention flickered between the rising elevator and me – but I knew the power my blood had over magical creatures.

*More to eat in the elevator—but **I'm** a tastier meal, aren't I?*

Sure enough, its decision was quickly made.

"Lord Elliott," she whispered. "...Good luck."

At my back, the rising platform scraped past the ceiling. *What did I say, Kinsey? I told you: '**We** never stood a chance.' With a little luck on my side... alone, perhaps **I** do...*

My quarterstaff, in hindsight, had been a stupid

weapon to choose with allies in the fray. I'd never trained in a group setting with it, and so the mistake was made. But they were all gone now, whisked to safety—and with those allies left the quick escape. Nothing else was left in this crystalline, glowing hell than the feral beast and me.

"Alright, you..." I steeled myself.

Its low snarl echoed in the empty chamber.

"Just the two of us now..." Both of us became hunter and prey; the tide could turn any moment. "No more distractions – nobody else to get hurt. Time to show me what you've got."

The tatzelwurm roared, lunging forward...

9
NIKKI

My madness flickered at the edges of my mind. It whispered sweet nothings to me like a lover in the dark, snuggled up on the pillow. Complicated but endearing, it was neither an entity nor a voice – it was a *feeling*, but I liked to imagine it sometimes.

I wondered what she looked like. That's right, she's a *she* to me. I never named her, though. *That* would have been crazy. But the personification of my madness was always there when I needed her, comforting me when my darkest moments came. She was my best friend for about a hundred years. I knew she only wanted what was best for me, but we had our differences. Even I had to admit that her methods were a tad dangerous, and I ignored the most irrationally chaotic of her suggestions.

I loved my madness.

My madness loved me.

But there was someone in my life – someone real, and tangible, bound in flesh and blood that I could physically reach. He was a flawed creature, and we rarely agreed, but he was someone whom I loved even more than my beautiful insanity.

And he needed me.

The soil of the Stonehold mainland crunched under my worn boots as I entered the village. It still surprised me how quickly I'd arrived. Within my hundred years away from the castle, chrysm technology had advanced at an unbelievable rate. Teleportation nodes were still in their infancy at the time, but their manageable drawbacks were now clearly a thing of the past.

What took over an hour of preparation a mere century before – teleporting across the sea – now took me mere seconds.

Even with my astonishment, I couldn't ignore the seductive whispers in my head, questioning why I'd come. THINK OF HOW HE'S TREATED YOU SINCE YOU'VE COME BACK. HE'S A FOOL. IGNORE THE DISTRESS SIGNAL. LEAVE HIM. LET HIM ACCEPT HIS FOOLISH FATE...

"No," I whispered to the air. "We need Elliott. He must stay alive. Leave him alone."

ARE YOU SURE? My madness knew better than to envy Elliott. The feeling inside hated neither him, nor how I still adored him. But this insanity was forever a part of me now. It had long since soaked down into my bones, always trying to coerce my mind into the abyss – and my brother was forever tied into the events that did it to me.

*Surely, you couldn't really blame me for relishing the chance to be **done** with him, after all this time...*

It was true. I couldn't.

Then let's turn around, and we can–

"Leave him alone," I snapped.

An unfamiliar voice called out. It was one of the miners. "Sorry? Leave *who* alone?"

I ignored the question.

"Is this Gransome Village?"

The miner peered at me curiously. "Of course it is. There's no other settlement for ages. Are you new to these parts?"

I approached him with a grin that clearly set him at unease. "Actually, yes..."

"Ah," he stumbled backwards. "Well then, I'm sure someone else can, well, you know, lend you a quick hand... seeing as you're lost and all..."

"Oh, I'm not lost," I planted a hand against the wall near him, peering evilly into his eyes. "Turns out, you guys have something of mine. Some*one*, if I'm being accurate..." My eyes squinted with a wicked glint. "And I'd very much like them back."

"Wh-who?"

I chuckled darkly. "Surely, you recognize me. My name is Nikki Craven, sister of Elliott Craven."

The miner visibly gulped.

"You're here for... for Lord Elliott?"

"That's right. That *Lord Elliott* of yours is kind of important to me. Now, I've come a very long way from Stonehold Castle... and let me be the first to put your fears to bed."

He looked relieved.

That was a mistake he wouldn't make again.

"If my older brother has been left in harm's way," I told him with an affectionate smile, "and I come to find out that it had *anything* to do with the people of this village..."

The miner shuddered under my stare.

"...The sun will rise over your *graves*..."

※

My new friend, the trembling old miner, wasted no time in introducing me to higher authorities.

"Lady Craven?" The village elder spoke in awe as I walked into some kind of hall. At least a dozen vampires were sulking about, all dressed in their boring old workers' garb. *This has to be where their adorable mining guild likes to have fun little chats about smacking rocks, or ripping stuff out from the ground, or murdering their sworn leader...* "This is quite the surprise. I had no idea that you were in this part of the hold."

"I swear," I ranted, "the next person who tries to make small talk with me while my brother is in danger gets thrown from atop Craven Keep."

Sure, the room was mostly silent before, but *now* the silence was so heavy in the air that you could almost cut it with a knife. *ACTUALLY, YOU HAVE A FEW ON YOU RIGHT NOW! I WONDER IF WE CAN—*

No, I snapped inwardly.

*Remember: concentrate on **Elliott**...*

"Looks like we're all on the same page now... So, since we're just getting to know each other, here's an idea... let's do team-building exercises! I know a really fun game that I like to call, *'What the Hell is Going On Here?* Winner gets a prize!" My leering face twisted around the miners while I searched for the weak link in the group. "Spoiler alert: the prize is that you don't have to find out what happens when I *really* lose it."

"Lord Craven descended underground," one of them quickly chirped up.

I turned on him. "We have a winner! Tell me more, and make it fast..."

"WHAT DO YOU MEAN, 'A MAGICAL CREATURE'?" I

yanked the wounded guard up to her feet, glaring down into her with my favorite smile. She looked terrified; that's how I knew it was working.

"*Which* magical creature?" I insisted.

The guard trembled in my grasp.

"Lady Craven!" The elder gasped. "Please, this guard is the only conscious one of the bunch that came back up from the mines! If we'd know you would scare her like this, I'd have never allowed you to see her!"

"It's a good thing you have no authority over me, then, isn't it?" I turned to him with a vicious glare. "Unless you *dare* question a Craven?"

"Of course not," The elder quieted down at that. "My sincerest apologies..."

I lowered my face sweetly to the guard.

"What is your name?"

"Kinsey," she choked.

"Kinsey," I repeated. *That's such a sweet name.* "Don't you worry... I'm not going to hurt you, my little Kinsey," I reassured her. "That is, unless you waste my time any further. If that's the plan, then let me know right now and we can start the song and dance—give me half an hour, I'll get the blades sharpened and we can have some *real* fun this morning..."

"Th-that won't be necessary, Lady Craven."

"Good," I grinned lovingly. "So tell me what I need to know, little bat."

The guard shuddered. "Lord Elliott told me I needed to know its name: *tatzelwurm*."

Even my madness silenced itself in horror.

"No," I gasped, releasing my grip on her out of blind astonishment. "That can't be... it *can't*..."

"It was... horrible," she groaned. "Face like a cat, body like a snake... gigantic... *murderous*... that hellish thing came at us like Death itself..."

*That's **definitely** a tatzelwurm – but how? How did one of them wind up underground?* Struggling to focus, my mind reeled as it tried to figure it out. *Tatzelwurms are mythical, malicious little snots, rare even in these parts... but they **hate** living in the dark!*

Their nesting habits, their prey, *everything* about them kept the spiteful creatures out of the caves and high in the peaks. They only ever crept near the roads when the pickings grew slim in their natural, mountainous habitats...

Still focused on the wounded guard, I glared indignantly over at the mines. "You're telling me, little bat, that you left my older brother down there *alone* with an adult goddamn tatzelwurm?!"

"He saved our lives. If it weren't for–"

I silenced Kinsey with a low snarl; afterward, I turned back to the winner of my earlier game, the one who had come in with the elder. It seemed his name was Pavric. "Get me down there."

"We can't risk bringing that thing up to—"

Taking a step closer, I whipped a dagger from its scabbard. Judging by the look on his face, the mere presence of it in my curled fist did plenty of the talking for me. "My brother, *your vampire lord,* is down there and probably dead by now."

I turned to the guard. "No thanks to you."

With a furious growl, I glanced at him again. "Now, you have the easiest job on the planet right now, don't you?" My madness pushed a loving, endearing smile across my face. "All you have to do is send me down there so I can take vengeance on that utter abomination, *so help me gods...*"

He looked unimpressed. "The beast's already killed half the guild, murdered a royal guard, and wounded many more. Forgive my skepticism, but what makes you think you can kill it?"

CLEARLY, NIKKI, THE BLADE'S NOT TALKING FAST ENOUGH, a dark whisper slid into my head. Smirking, I obeyed its compulsion and grabbed the stupid worker by the throat, slamming him hard against the wall.

His eyes bugged in surprise as he instinctively kicked around his feet, but the effort was useless. My vampire lord blood gave me the strength to hold his choking body up against the wall, a few feet above the ground.

"Because I have *hunted* them," I snarled viciously.

Before he could respond, we were interrupted by

scattered cries of surprise. I growled, released him from my clutches, and hesitantly turned to face the entrance of the Dawning Mines.

Must have lured it up to the surface, my madness observed. *You have the blood of the vampire lords in your veins... and the thing's all riled up now, isn't it? It probably noticed you...*

Mentally, I was pulled in two directions.

First, I had to acknowledge that my brother was probably dead. The very thought of a world without him buried my twisted heart in sorrow, no matter how my thoughts contorted over him – drawn between love and distrust.

But on the other hand, this demented, chaotic thing inside me *always* loved an excuse to spill warm blood, and there was never a better reason for wanton violence than the thought of *revenge*...

As I marched towards the gaping maw of the caverns, my hand ripped an axe from its supports. Wood planks splintered as I spun the axe to a rest on my shoulder; the taste of blood was already on my tongue. *If my brother is truly gone,* I thought as I embraced my lust for destruction, *why not cleave its head from its body? The beast must pay the ultimate price for **daring** to cross my loved ones...*

But that's not what I saw coming.

The axe slipped from my fingers to the dirt.

No, the madness groaned in defeat. *How? How is this even possible? Why couldn't it have–*

"Shut up," I snapped at the voice. By the kinds of looks I got, I blurted that out a little too loudly, but you know what? Screw them.

A confused voice rang out. "Nikki?"

Elliott stumbled forward from the shadows. I rushed forward to his bloody body as my brother dropped to his knees. A mangled quarterstaff hit the dirt beside him; on his other side, he dropped the head of the tatzelwurm.

He gasped wearily. "It's done."

"That's right, brother," I cradled his head to my chest. Elliott was in no condition to stride back to the chrysm node, but that was perfectly fine. *I'd carry your battered body back across the sea over my* **shoulder** *if I had to.* "You've done so well. Rest now, my dearest Elliott. Let me bring us back home."

"The tatzelwurm..." He grunted painfully.

"It's dead," I smiled proudly. "You won."

"No, it..." Something bothered him, even in his shock. "You don't understand... it was the beast's eyes... when I killed it... they glowed *violet...*"

Elliott's weak, trembling gaze darkened.

"Nikki... you *know*... what that *means*..."

With those words, he collapsed forward—his weary body little more than dead weight now—into my embrace. I held my dearest brother like that for a few painfully short minutes, savouring being this close to him again after all this time apart.

Violet eyes, the madness whispered in my ear. *That means that the tatzelwurm didn't come here of its own volition. It was purposefully **brought** here...*

Or worse, I agreed angrily. **Summoned...**

My heart seized in my chest.

There were only a few places left in the world with that kind of power, and *none* of them were in Stonehold. *I think I need to talk to that bloody sorceress again...* The deck needed to be stacked quicker, because it was clear to me that our enemies had just made their first move.

I lifted my resolute face to the rising dawn.

"The war begins..."

10

CLARA

I'd asked Sabine to put me back to sleep, once the others had gotten me hydrated. After I awoke this time and slept off some of the lingering pain, the others watching over me re-hydrated me from the start. The light was bearable to my eyes now, and it didn't feel like my body was burning alive inside.

I didn't have to ask what happened to Elliott.

He lied unconscious in the nearest bunk.

I was sitting upright in the medical bed with a cup of therapeutic, steaming tea in my hands. The others hovered nearby as I quietly watched Elliott sleep; my soul felt heavy with heartache.

"How long has he been this way?" I asked.

Seated in a chair by his liege, Wilhelm barely moved an inch as his eyes flickered over to me. "All day. That darling, *utterly* demented sister of his brought Lord

Elliott back to the castle like this. Seems the workers on the mainland didn't see any point in mentioning that *something* in the mines had been picking them off, one by one." The guard turned to his resting boss with a mournful glance. "It certainly explains the rumoured slowdowns in chrysm mining. Frankly, he's lucky to be alive."

I took another tea sip. "Where is Nikki now?"

He shrugged limply. "No idea."

Viktor walked over to Elliott's side and gazed at his vital signs on the beeping machines. The devices didn't look anything at all like the ones I'd seen back home... but this vampiric world, and its strange technology, was far weirder than mine.

"I can't believe it," he grunted despondently. "We *finally* get one of you up, and then the other drops." Looking up at me, he shook his head in resignation. "You two are a ridiculous pair."

"Heh," I grinned halfheartedly. "I guess so."

Asarra hadn't spoken a word. She was staring off into space, like all royal guards did when they wanted to ignore the effects of feeling time pass. *Of course, these three used to **be** royal guards...* I had it in my head to talk to Elliott about the barbaric procedure that gave them this power, but a lot had happened in the last few days.

And now there was this.

"What day is it?" I suddenly asked.

"Uh, Tuesday," Viktor answered.

"Oh." I chuckled morosely, disappearing back into my cup of tea. "Happy birthday to me."

Asarra snapped to awareness and glanced my way; the disbelief in her voice only enhanced that strange, Eastern European accent I loved so much. "It is your birthday? How interesting. Why did you not say anything?"

"As you may recall, my pretty little friend, she *just* woke up," Wilhelm demurely chuckled.

"Oh, but of course," the vampiric guardian blinked with her typically stoic expression. "How many years do you have now, Clara?"

I frowned. "Today makes seventeen."

By now, it didn't really surprise me that everyone within earshot was stunned to hear this. By their terms, I was *incredibly* young and comparatively mature for it. On a fundamental level, though, our lifespans were radically different. The numbers just happened to be greatly skewed in my favor.

From what the Craven siblings told me over a feast one night, birth through vampiric puberty lasted over a century, though the vampires might physically be in what a human would consider their *twenties* for most of that. To these people, someone of my nature being only seventeen years old was *completely* out of the norm.

"Seventeen years old... well, I'll be damned." Wilhelm

whistled while shaking his head. "Leave it to Lord Elliott to like them young..."

Asarra smacked him up the back of the head.

"Ow! What was *that* for?!"

"Do not be crude," the female guard grunted. "Show more respect to your master."

At the sound of my uncontrollable laughter, both of the vampires quizzically glanced my way. "I'm sorry guys, I know I shouldn't..." I forced out between laughs, "but this entire thing is just all so ridiculous that I can't help myself..."

Gradually, the room lit up with smiling faces. It seemed nobody, even the no-nonsense nurses, could deny how strange this all was.

"He's okay, though?" I looked fondly down at Elliott Craven. His frozen, placid face was locked into a quiet, brooding sleep. "Nobody's panicked about him since I've woken up, so I didn't think he was in any real trouble..."

A nearby nurse wiped her hands with a rag as she fretted over him. "Lord Craven will be fine. His injuries, while severe, aren't anything that we can't fix. He should be up by morning."

"Oh," I sadly noted. "He'll miss the whole day, then. Well, as long as he's safe and healthy."

The Knightly Trio shared a look, but I wasn't paying any attention. I climbed down from my bed and sat down next to his. I took Elliott's hand in both of mine, stroking it endearingly. It was so cold, and hard like stone. But the flesh was softer than I'd thought – hard, yet forgiving. I imagined that to be much like Elliott himself: hardened and stiffened by his experiences and responsibilities, but ultimately malleable and receptive.

I guess, maybe, there aren't so many differences between the vampire lord and I, I quietly wondered. *Not if his hand can feel like this. He certainly doesn't **feel** like a statue. Why, Elliott even feels like he could be a regular person...*

Nobody said a word. I didn't notice if anyone was watching as I leaned over the resting vampire and planted a kiss on his forehead.

I rose from Elliott's side. After I climbed back onto the side of my bed and scooped up my tea, I turned back to the rest of them. "It's clear to me that a lot's happened since I went under. Tell me everything."

It didn't take long to update me.

I shook my head. "It's hard to believe that our cold, calculating Elliott can be so reckless..."

The guards went quiet. Something in the air felt unsaid; right before I could point it out, Viktor turned to me with a glum expression.

"He hasn't been himself since you fell under."

"I... don't understand."

"You're a smart one," Wilhelm replied calmly. "Lord Elliott has been utterly distraught since you started your little *audition* for the coffin. To be honest, I think he blames himself." He turned to the resting vampire lord, sighing. "I've never heard of him acting so brashly. I almost didn't believe it, but I've seen his behaviour lately... and how he would only leave your side when his duties commanded it as necessary."

"He was *here?*"

"Well, either quietly sitting around in here, or sulking about out there," Wilhelm nodded at the opaque glass wall nearby. It nearly obstructed the view of the outside hallway. "Knowing him, our master would be embarrassed if he had any idea that we could see him out there."

"Lord Elliott was always here," Asarra agreed. "Always watching over his comatose girl."

I didn't know what to think of that.

Well, that's not *entirely* true.

My feelings on Elliott were complicated – and *that* was putting it mildly. In the weeks building up to my sudden arrival here, I'd dreamt of him every night. Cloaked in shadows, only a silhouette and a pair of glowing eyes, Elliott Craven entered my nightmares to save me from a terrible danger.

Imagine my utter surprise when I came face-to-face with him, flesh and blood...

TRIALS OF THE VAMPIRE

My attention averted to Sabine. The sorceress who had put me under the spell to begin with was buried in a spellbook nearby, deep in study. When she noticed me watching, she looked up.

"You haven't said very much," I noticed with a faint smile. "How've you been taking all of this? You arrived just in time for everything to really hit the wall... that must have been stressful."

Softly, Sabine closed the hardback book in her hands. "As a sorceress, I am used to the unusual. But what's happened here is beyond me."

"What, the comatose thing?"

"Yes, that. The only reasonable explanation is that you must be inherently resistant to magic..." Her eyes went strangely dark. *Did I just imagine that, or is she—* "However, that is quite impossible. There isn't a creature on Earth that can withstand magic – not without the further interference of *other* magic, of course."

"I'm not *from* Earth," I politely reminded her. "Well, at least not *this* Earth. I have my own one, somewhere else."

The sorceress seemed to consider that.

"I must speak with you alone soon. There are some tests I'd like to perform, and a few theories I have to rectify..."

"Of course," I smiled. "Whatever you need."

For a moment, I thought her eyes returned to that

dark glint. But nobody else seemed to notice, and it was gone again so fast that I thought I was just seeing things.

Something about it reminded me of a dream.

I was overwhelmed with a flash of memories. *My grandmother was walking me along a beach, in a distant world without colour...*

"Are you alright, Clara?"

I glanced up. Wilhelm's concerned face filled my vision, and I nodded with a displaced smile. "Yeah. Sorry, I just remembered a dream I had..."

"A dream? Looked serious."

"What do you mean?"

Viktor was nearby. "You stopped responding. Looked like you were about to pass out." He gave a teasing smile, a rarity for him. "We've had quite enough of that, if you could possibly spare us the trouble there..."

"Oh, of course," I distantly nodded.

That's when I felt something unusual and unfamiliar brushing against my collarbone. It occurred to me that the sensation had bothered me for quite some time. In fact, it had subtly been right there ever since I woke back up – but I'd been ignoring it until now.

"Wait... what is...?" My hand clasped around something cold and metallic on my skin; I gasped as I looked up, making eye contact with Sabine. The sorceress curiously watched me, perched in her seat with cat-like interest.

"What is it?" She leaned closer. "...Clara?"

You mustn't tell them, I remembered a voice.

Hide it from them as long as you can...

"Oh... nothing," I smiled. "I just thought... but no, that was the dream again. It's nothing."

She looked a little disappointed. "Oh, I see."

I withdrew my fingers from below my throat, hiding how they trembled in disbelief... because there, against my skin under my shirt, rested the necklace that my grandmother gave me the last time I saw her, when I was a young child.

And I'd lost it over a decade before.

11
ELLIOTT

In the dreariness of a deep and dark slumber, before my eyes finally flicked open, I was partly aware of the following things.

Nearby, a machine beeped with my vitals.

There were *three* other vampires in the room.

Two of them fretted over the machine.

The *last* was...

"Of all people," I grunted in slight pain and irritation, "I'm surprised that it's *you*."

"Welcome back, Elliott."

I opened my eyes to see Lorelei Craven sitting beside me, one leg hung over the other. I noticed how she held her hands clasped in her lap.

"Nervousness doesn't suit you, Mother."

She scoffed, turning away from me. "It seems your

experiences are making you arrogant. I don't recall raising an conceited prince."

"You *barely* raised us," I replied.

"Stonehold needed me."

"Yes. It did. But it didn't need you every hour of every day. Had you been a little more attentive to your children, perhaps your daughter wouldn't have, well..."

Her eyes flared. "Elliott, don't you dare."

"I will 'dare' how I see fit." I slowly rose up to a seated position. "You wanted me to be a vampire lord? Now you've got one." The pain caught up to me, and I winced. *My wounds may be superficially gone, but everything still aches,* I thought to myself disparagingly.

"You are thinking of the creature," she noted.

"Yes. The pain lingers."

"That would be the poison," one of the nurses helpfully replied. "The tatzelwurm must have struck you with a poisonous swipe at some point. We extracted almost all the contaminants from your bloodstream during treatment. Were you any lesser a vampire, Lord Craven, the attack very likely would have killed you." She turned away. "In fact, that's precisely what took your guard's life. His body just couldn't metabolize the venom to the extent yours can."

I grunted. "And the others?"

"They're resting." She motioned over to a row of four

occupied beds, faraway on the other side of the medical bay, on the other side of a glass barrier; another nurse diligently tended to them. "Resting, but alive and safe."

"Didn't realize a tatzelwurm was lurking out there," I groaned painfully as I met Lorelei's gaze.

She looked positively furious, and I steeled myself for her anger. "What you did was suicidal," she spoke coolly. "If you had gotten yourself killed, the hold would have descended into total anarchy. Elliott, you are *far* too valuable to the safety and prosperity of Stonehold to jeopardize yourself in such a way."

"Why, that almost sounds affectionate..."

She glowered, but ignored my sarcasm. "The moment that you knew the truth, you should've sent over for reinforcements. Instead, you chose to play hero for the hold." She bitterly shook her head. "They may not like you, but they *cannot* afford to lose you."

"Might I remind you that they don't like me because *you never taught me how to lead,*" I angrily rebuked her. "Three hundred and fifty years, and you barely taught me the essentials. How did you think I would perform, then?"

She ignored my outburst. "You faced an adult tatzelwurm. One of your guards must be buried. The others have been deeply traumatized. There were *other ways* to solve the crisis. For gods' sakes, Elliott, you had a capable sorceress in the castle! But you *had* to take the quick, undiplomatic route. You're making the same bloody mistakes that *she* did, Elliott. You can't expect to simply *overpower* all of your problems. You're just as bad as Fio–"

At the slip-up, my mother haughtily clenched her jaw and lifted her chin, turning away.

That's just like you, snapping to silence. Whenever I need help, you always hold your damned tongue...

Lorelei meaningfully glanced at the nurses—she clearly wanted them to leave. My medical staff turned to me for some form of guidance, and I nodded.

"Lord Craven," the senior began with a start, "I can't say I advise you to dismiss us. With all due respect, you've only *just* woken back–"

"Leave," I commanded, verbally this time.

The nurses reluctantly gathered a few things and left the two of us alone in the medical bay. I followed their steps with my stare; once we were alone again, I turned back to my mother.

"Your concern is touching," I snarked. "If you wonder why I left the sorceress here, I put Sabine to work looking over Clara. I have Sebastian in the library, searching other tomes, but Sabine was left here to either pull her back from her coma, or find a way to reverse the spell altogether..."

"A spell *you* ordered, with no testing."

"Because there was a *foreign vampire lord in the castle!*" I snapped. "Or have you already forgotten? Akachi Azuzi came here, to the Isle of Obsidian, searching for our human visitor. It will be only a matter of time before he grows bolder – or the *others* do!"

"Elliott, you fool, it means nothing if you kill her in the process, or worse – suppose that you get *yourself* killed trying to solve it. What will happen to Stonehold then?"

"Do not begin to criticize me when you offer nothing in return. You refuse to give counsel, you deny me any advice... if you truly think you can do better, I will *gladly* offer you the opportunity. Take your bloody throne back and rule the people like you did for six hundred years."

"That will not happen."

"Then help me, or *stay out of my way*."

"Hmph." Lorelei shifted her gaze with a blink. "Tell me, if you won't use your sorceress, what do you plan on doing with her?"

"I have not decided," I replied.

"Your answer inspires such confidence."

My patience was running thin. "She has only been here a few days. I would consider finding her a place in the castle, but I sense something in her."

"I do too," Lorelei noted. "Ambition."

"Sabine jumped at the call. She quite obviously

desires a place in the Stonehold Court," I observed coolly. "I have not yet decided what to make of her, and require a little more time to figure her out. Especially since I have been... *preoccupied,* these last few days."

"The woman is a powerful magic-caster, to be sure. Perhaps she could make an equally powerful ally in the times to come. Perhaps not."

"Precisely," I nodded. "And yet, I hear whispers that she privately meets with my deranged sister after dark. Servants have seen them speaking in dark alcoves and in abandoned parts of the castle. I wonder if it is wise to keep either of them around..."

"Elliott, they are both useful."

"Yet they scheme, where they think I cannot find them. But I know you have a point. I *do* see how useful they are," I reminded her coldly. "My sister has spent the last century wandering the mainland – living among the people, listening to their stories. For all her insanity, Nikki proves indispensible in her survival knowledge and skill with reconnaissance...

"Whereas, keeping a sorceress at my disposal with Sabine's skillset has uses even *I* can't fathom. It would be imprudent to send her away, instead of putting her to work as a member of my circle. If she craves a spot at the table, perhaps the path of least resistance—simply *giving it to her*—would keep the sorceress... predictable. But how?"

"As I first took the throne, magic was unrefined to an astonishing degree, outside of *private* institutions," Lorelei noted distractedly. "Distrust ran rampant. There was no place for a magician in the court of a vampire lord, and I chose to rule with only the minimal advisors —namely, the one you so callously ignore." Her eyes narrowed. "And so I chose to abolish the system to put them in place." She lifted an eyebrow. "But there *is* a way to circumvent that."

It occurred to me that Lorelei was actually being helpful, but I had no intentions of jinxing it. "What do you mean?"

"The vassal system," she noted obliquely.

"Right..." I'd nearly forgotten about it. "It's been a long time. Tell me more about it."

Lorelei blinked oddly; her eyes looked strange for a moment, and she turned back to me. "It isn't important for now. Hard to believe, perhaps, but I did not come here to reminisce over the past and its flaws. There is no use in that."

Well. **That** *certainly lasted long. I knew this was too good to be true, a Lorelei who actually dispensed advice...*

"Fine," I groaned irritably, making a point to venture into the library to ask Sebastian about this *vassal* system, as soon as I was done speaking to this insufferable woman. "Why *did* you come here, then? Just to taunt me further with your disapproval at my choices?"

She turned to me coldly. "I must leave soon."

The words struck me like freezing water. *Go? After throwing me beneath the weight of this entire hold and watching me flounder for a year, you dare to... simply **leave** me?*

I knew she'd never answer to that.

"Where are you going?" I asked instead.

Lorelei sighed, but her demeanor didn't lose a scrap of self-importance. "I must go out to the Far Reaches to fulfill my role in what comes next..."

"What comes *next*?"

Lorelei sighed, but her eyes stayed on mine. "There are many things we must discuss together, but I don't have much time. In a few days, I'll need to be on the mainland, and there are preparations I must attend to first."

"Convenient that I woke up now, then."

She chuckled without a single ounce of joy in her throat. "If you had taken any longer, I would have had your nurses pull you back prematurely. My time is valuable right now."

"Somehow, I'm not even remotely surprised. Always such a caring mother, you were."

Lorelei switched her hanging leg for the other and clasped her hands tighter. When she leaned forward, her face lit up with an unnatural smile. The sight sent shivers down my spine.

"My son, of the many lessons you will have to learn,

one is to forgo your obsession with getting in the last word... now, would you like to finally learn *why* I gave up the throne?"

I told her yes.

It wasn't long before I regretted it.

12
CLARA

It felt good to get out and stretch my legs. It seemed as if I'd been stuck in bed for *days!*

Which... was technically true.

The Knightly Trio led me around Craven Keep for a few hours. They kept me restricted to areas away from any of the servants; I found my way to the nearest balcony and gazed up at the beautiful half-night sky outside.

"You seem to love that sky," Viktor told me.

"Of course I do! It's nothing like what we have back on my world." I pointed up to the way that the stars shone through the daylight – their sky always let a little night through the air, mostly in the highest reaches. "Like that wonderful cosmos up there. You see those purples and pinks? That's better than anything us humans get. We have to wait until night falls to see the stars."

"Really?" Asarra asked. "That is so boring."

Wilhelm happily smirked. "I know, right? I mean, who has the patience to wait for..."

When I noticed that his words trailed had off, I pulled my attention down from the sky. He, as well as the other two, stared behind us. I followed his gaze to the figure quietly watching nearby and almost squealed with delight.

Elliott Craven leaned against the doorway, his arms folded. As our eyes met, a sly smile began to cross his face, and he unfolded his arms to take a few swaggering steps my way.

The sight of him stirred something warm and tender within me. I could feel it rising from deep in my heart. *He looks so effortlessly handsome...*

The vampire narrowed his eyes at the others with a slight grin.

Viktor swallowed. "We should..."

I felt a pair of strong hands on my shoulders. Wilhelm snickered cheerily at my back. "Alright kids, have some fun. And you!" He feigned his sternest, paternal voice at his boss. "You have her back here by ten o'clock, or I'll have your throat!"

Elliott's smile darkened. "Oh?"

My guardian chuckled nervously. "Right... oh,

wouldn't you just look at the time? I have to run. Believe I left my, uh, my *cat* on..."

I bit back laughter as the room cleared around us. The Knightly Trio slunk from sight; they took positions just outside the balcony door as it closed behind them.

Elliott and I were finally reunited.

Reunited, and *alone*...

"You're up earlier than expected," I smiled.

"Yes, Lorelei came to talk to me. As you might imagine, she is quite skilled at getting my blood boiling... but enough about that. You worried me," he smiled softly.

"I know I did, and I'm sorry."

His smirk devilishly lit up his face. "I know it wasn't your fault. "

"Of course not," I grinned. "It was *yours*." The smile faded from Elliott's face, and I laughed even harder. "I'm just kidding. We *both* know you were just trying to protect me from the dangers of your castle. I wasn't safe here."

I stepped closer. "But I am now. Now that I'm here, with you."

Elliott tilted his chin and blinked once; with the warm, peaceful expression that slipped across his face, and the love reflected in his eyes, it was more than a small sign of endearment.

"I haven't been myself without you, Clara."

My eyes trailed to his strong, capable arms, hanging

down by his sides. Gingerly, I placed my fingertips along his pale skin, running them up his firm muscles and onto his shoulders. As our bodies pulled together, my arms settled around his neck and I felt his hands on my hips.

Without a single syllable, Elliott and I slowly swayed to music that wasn't playing. We had our own silent sonata together; our feet moved to the trailing rhythm of the tranquility. Of all the times in my life, this moment was the one that felt the realest. Beneath that impossible sky, everything seemed snapped into place, all where it belonged.

"Did they tell you?" I quietly asked him.

"Tell me what?"

My chin nuzzled into his hard shoulder. "It's my birthday today."

I heard him suck in a small breath. "Is it now?"

"That's right," I chuckled. "Seventeen."

"Seventeen years old..." He pondered it in his head, and I wondered what he thought of that. *Safe to say, that's a pretty strong age difference...*

"How old is that?" Elliott asked. "Compared to the rest of an average human's lifetime, remind me where that age falls... give me context."

I smiled against him, enjoying the feeling of our closeness as we moved together in harmony. "I love that you thought to ask that. You could've just drawn your own conclusions, but you didn't."

"Of course not," he replied kindly. "If I want to truly be a capable ruler, I'll always require perspective outside my own. I must always ask questions, even when the answers seem plainly obvious, because it will *never* matter how smart I might be if I entirely rely on my own experiences."

He extended me out in a swaying movement, separating us by all but a hand; with a deft motion, he pulled me back in.

"Context is everything, Clara. Tell me yours."

He completely enamoured me. The tales of his utter recklessness against the monster fell to the wayside as I gazed into his youthful eyes.

"Seventeen years old..." I paused to think how I could word it to make the most sense to Elliott. "It varies around the world, but I'm considered an adult back home in England. Have been for a year. One more year, I can even order my own alcohol. And that's how much longer I have in my education before I'd have to choose: go into debt but stay in higher schooling, or try to join the workforce..."

It was getting harder to remember the details, to my total surprise. *I've really only been here for a few weeks, but now my life back home feels like a distant dream...*

"...By now, I might even be married in other cultures. I might even have a child. Two hundred years ago, I'd have at *least* one or two at seventeen."

"A child?" He blinked, surprised.

"Yes, is that weird?"

"Children are rare," he replied casually. "How do your people determine whether or not the next generation of children should be born?"

"What do you mean, 'determine'?"

"Surely, there is a system. How else could your people expect to keep the world population from exploding well beyond its means?"

"...They don't." The idea perplexed me. "Partially why we have so many of us around the world. Well, I *say* that, but a few countries have tried it. China was one of them."

"China?"

"Yes, it's a major world superpower. It's probably one of the closer things to a 'hold' that we have, to use your words. China is an ancient civilization in the modern day, and one of our largest economic nations."

"Where is it?"

"It's a large chunk of Southern Asia," I clarified, "north of the peninsula and spread out below Russia." When I saw his confused look, I chuckled with faint recollection. "Right. You know, I almost forgot for a moment – different worlds. Different divisions of the world geography. Let me think, I have to remember what your maps looked like... oh yeah!" I smiled up at him with warmth in my eyes.

"You call that place 'Alevorra' here. It's a pretty name."

"Ah yes, Alevorra," he repeated. "A sprawling tropical paradise, and home to a great civilization. The largest city on the planet is there—a great city of stone temples and powerful relics."

"Stone temples? Like Angkor Wat?"

"Angkor Wat?"

"Yeah, that's the capital of, oh, what did they call that again..." *It's right on the tip of my tongue. Such a fascinating culture, and one that they have almost no records for—* "The Khmer Empire. That's right, a huge Asian civilization that disappeared a long time ago. Most of the temples are buried in the ground now, but we still have the decaying ruins and sanctuaries of Angkor Wat to go by..."

"Sounds like you're basically talking about present-day Alevorra. The vampires out in those parts live in a lush, thriving jungle where the air is too hot and wet for most of us. I suppose it's somewhat telling that so many there have become natural seafarers over the millennia..."

We continued to sway with our own music, and I held him just a little tighter. "You know, I've come to love these little differences between both our worlds. I enjoy hearing you talk about the rest of these vampiric civilizations. They're so exotic."

"Exotic, yes." His expression clouded for a moment. "Exotic, but highly dangerous."

"Oh, surely they can't all be *that* bad," I spoke with what I hoped was a charming air. "After all, there are still vampires living there, right? Were they all *that* dangerous, wouldn't half of them be long dead?"

"The vampires themselves are a large part of the problem," he clarified pensively. "The deeper into the great wilds you venture, the thicker the magic you find. Scholars all across the world have theories about the longstanding effects. There are schools of thought that living in such a strong level of magic, especially for your entire life, does unforeseen things to the mind."

My mouth moved before I realized I spoke. "Is that why you fear the other vampire lords?"

Elliott stiffened.

"I didn't mean— I'm sorry, I—"

"No," he replied contemplatively. "I fear them because they are great and powerful creatures, far more dangerous than any mere *tatzelwurm*..."

He disappeared into thought for a moment.

"No," I whispered softly. I pulled his face back towards mine with a light finger beneath his chin. "Stay here with me, Elliott."

The vampire smiled.

It was the most handsome thing I'd ever seen.

"Don't worry, my dear Clara. I'm right here. I don't intend on being anywhere else."

"Good," I grinned. "You'd better not."

We pulled closer, Elliott and I, still swaying to the soundless music in our heads. Soon, there was nothing separating our bodies as we lovingly held each other close. We moved together as one, with the only distance between us being our lips.

He leaned down into my smiling face.

With his kiss, even that distance was gone.

13

ELLIOTT

Clara's lips were like the softest velvet, warmly filled with life, as they brushed against my own.

I didn't want them to ever part.

The kiss grew in strength as I felt the hushed whimper in her voice. In her humanity, she was such a fragile, endearing little creature. *I know not what kind of spell you have cast over me, my dearest Clara, but don't you dare abandon it now.*

When we parted lips, she gazed into my eyes. Her vulnerability shone through like the brightest light in an otherwise cold and looming darkness.

"How strange..." she whispered slyly. "If I didn't know any better, I'd say you don't seem so desperate for my blood anymore..."

I blinked. I'd almost forgotten about that.

"No," I murmured. "I suppose I don't."

"Then you know what that means."

My smile widened. "The spell..."

Clara's eyes lit up with charming wonder. "It *worked*, Elliott. It was worth it. I'm truly *safe* now."

No words have ever brought me such joy.

I pulled her into another warm, loving kiss. She cooed with delight as I held her close, tightly holding her warm, soft body against mine. My lips were addicted to her; I pulled them back less than half an inch, only to press them down again.

"Oh god, Elliott..."

We kissed long and hard, holding each other as if we were young, naïve lovers. Of course, that's exactly what we were – wrapped up in the sudden strength of our bond. This impossible thing had happened to pull us both together from across the barriers between worlds.

It seemed fated, she and I.

After a few moments of our powerful kissing, I felt pangs of resistance. Clara pulled away with a sheepish frown, averting her gaze.

My heart trembled. I'd never known *anyone* I'd be willing to let have any power over me, let alone over my *heart*. Yet, it was increasingly clear that I'd already done that very thing, whether or not I'd realized it. Seeing the pained look on her face tugged at my heartstrings, pulling in ways I could never have imagined. "What's the matter, Clara? Was that too much?"

"It's not that," she murmured.

"Oh? I don't think I underst–"

Her stomach's loud growl interrupted us.

Together, we both bit down on our lips before descending into laughter. Without another word, I scooped her into my embrace and guided her back into Craven Keep. As her three guardians snapped to alertness and followed us down the stairs, I pushed Clara onward to the dining hall...

※

AFTER MAKING CERTAIN THEY ALL UNDERSTOOD IT WAS a very special night, I had my kitchen staff whip up a celebratory feast. My servants toiled quickly and diligently. Soon, our head server promised us an endless selection of truly delicious food – and that was just the first spread of appetizer plates.

Once I confirmed the selections and sent him back into the kitchen to relay them, Clara turned to me with a gasp.

"Oh Elliott, that's far too much!"

"Nonsense," I smirked. "It's your birthday."

Clara smiled and leaned closer. "Do you think it's possible, you know, before they start bringing the food out... do you think that we could have Nikki eat with us again?"

My eyebrow lifted. "What do you mean?"

"Well..." Her face saddened. "If it's too much to ask, I understand, but... it's been a really long time since I've had a proper birthday party. Not since my parents died, at any rate."

"A birthday party?"

"Yeah." Her eyebrows rose. "Wait..."

I shrugged. "What's a 'birthday party'?"

Clara gasped. "You don't celebrate *birthdays?*"

"Not really," I politely shrugged. "We all have so many birthdays: hundreds of them, in fact. Never particularly seen much reason to treat them as anything other than just another day..."

Her expression moved me. "That's so sad."

"Tell me, what is it about birthdays that make them so important in your world?"

She thought on that for a moment. "You have to remind yourself, Elliot, that our lifespans are so much shorter than yours. Our generations come and go more rapidly, and our families spread out faster as a result. We use birthdays as a way to bring our loved ones back together to celebrate what we enjoy most about each other."

"What do you do? Is there a ritual?"

"A *ritual?*" she laughed. "Well, sometimes there is a birthday party. Your friends and family come around to visit and, well, I guess they sort of feast in your honor..."

I listened raptly. *This sounds quite like nothing I'd ever heard of before...* A celebration of oneself was well beyond any party I'd ever heard of – at least, not unless one was an especially narcissistic and vainglorious vampire.

"Then there's a birthday cake," she continued.

"Birthday cake?" I asked curiously, brushing aside my thoughts on vampiric vanity. *I'm always looking for an opportunity for **cake**...* "How is it different from any regular cake?"

"Well, someone brings it out to you with a ton of tiny, lit candles up on top. Some do it with one thick, squat candle, shaped in the number of your age. Personally, I think the first way is a lot better. One candle for every year... laid out in whatever way looks best."

Clara smiled when she saw what must have been a captivated, amused expression on my face, but she barely skipped a beat.

"Although, on second thought I guess there *is* something of a ritual to it. When the person brings your cake out, everyone sings a birthday song for you. When it's over, they have you make a wish and blow out the candles..."

"A birthday song?"

"That's right," she nodded enthusiastically. "Here, it goes something like this:

Happyyy birrthdaay tooo yooouu
Happyyy birrthdaay tooo yooouu
Happyyy birthday, dear...yoour-naaaame...
Happyyy birrthdaay to youuuuu

My eyebrow rose. "That's standard?"

"Oh sure," she laughed. "What you just heard is one of the most famous songs across the whole world. It's probably sung *thousands* of times a day in countries — er, holds — all over Earth."

I sounded out the words in my head. *Quite a simple little song,* I noticed, *with barely any lyrics to it. But it puts such warmth in my heart...*

"After the song's over, like I said, you make a wish and blow out the candles. Then, everybody starts handing you your birthday gifts. While you thank them and open up your presents, the cake is split up and shared among all the guests. From there on, it's basically just whatever the rest of the night calls for."

I stroked my chin. "Fascinating..."

Clara shook her head in utter disbelief. "Do you guys *seriously* not do anything like that here? How is it that you don't celebrate something so simple as *birthdays?*"

"Like I said..." I leaned back in my chair with a small grin. "I suppose our kind just doesn't see much of a point to it. Consider, for instance, that part with the candles. I mean, can you *imagine?* Most cakes would have *hundreds* of candles!"

"That's why some are made with the single candle shaped like their age," she reminded me.

"I see." A mischievous plan started to form in the back of my head. "Well, if you really want my sister here at the table, I should inform the staff. If you'll excuse me a moment..."

She narrowed her eyes. "Why not just have a servant tell them? You *hate* getting back up once you're settled in at the table."

Clever girl, I thought to myself.

"After all the excitement last night, I'm eager to stretch my legs a little. That, and they'd never expect me to waltz in. I like a good surprise."

"Are you... are you sure that you're okay?"

"What? Oh, yes. Of course," I reassured her.

"It's just... if you aren't well, I don't want you up and over-exerting yourself, Elliott."

"It's your birthday, and I'm not missing it. I'll be fine, my dear. The nurses of the castle aren't on my pay without good reason. Now, if you'll let me speak to the staff..."

Clara looked unconvinced. I planted a peck on her forehead, and she offered up a smile.

"That's right. There's my girl."

Her face oddly reddened at that.

Once I strolled through the servant's doors to the kitchen, I started carefully forming my plan. Distractedly, I grabbed the first chef I saw.

"L-Lord Craven? Is everything alright?"

"Well, that depends. Do you happen to have a cake on hand? I have something in mind for it..."

"A cake?" She gave a glance over her shoulder. "Well, yes we do, but why would you—"

"Good," I smirked. "What flavor?"

"Your favorite. Chocolate."

"Excellent. What about icing? Candles?"

"Well, yes! Of course!"

"Fantastic. Now, I'm going to sneak out the other way and talk to the guards – I want some people tracked down and sent over to the feast, so you'll need to cook a little extra of everything. You should go ahead and have the kitchen take a little longer than usual with the food, just to give them all time to arrive... but that's not all. There is a certain *song* the servers will need to be taught. It's a simple one, very difficult to mess up..."

Heroically, the perplexed cook tried to hide her complete exasperation. It didn't escape my notice that all her nearby kitchen staff pretended to focus on their work, thinly hiding their total amusement. "Lord Craven, with all due respect, what is this all about? Are you quite alright?"

My face erupted into a devilish grin.

"In all your centuries, my dear, have you ever heard of a strange ritual called a *birthday* party...?"

14

CLARA

Right before the appetizers started arriving, there came a loud, impatient knocking from the nearby gate. Elliott suspiciously tried to hide a smile as he nodded over to the stationed guard.

Nikki and Lorelei wandered into the room.

"Oh, hi!" I grinned happily up at them. "I was hoping to see you soon. And Miss Lorelei, this is a surprise. I'm glad you could make it too!"

"Of course," Nikki grinned evilly. "You *know* I like to play with my food before I eat it..." When she looked over my shoulder at Elliott's face, her demented grin slipped away. "Oh, fine. Alright, I guess I *did* promise to be on better behaviour..."

Lorelei remained as distant as ever.

"I'm sorry if I alarmed you," I told her.

"Why would you have *alarmed* me?"

"Well, the coma comes to mind..."

"Oh, *that?*" She laughed conceitedly. "No, that was my son's concern, not mine. So long as you didn't drop dead on us, I wasn't' that..."

I didn't know what face Elliott was making, but it seemed to have the same effect as it had on Nikki. To my surprise, the notoriously apathetic Lorelei Craven turned to me with a renewed smile on her face. "I am pleased that you're safe, Clara. Welcome back to us."

"It's a delight to be back."

"Ah yes," she smirked. "The manners... how I always seem to forget your unfailing *manners*..."

"Well, what are you two standing around for? Take a seat," Elliott motioned to the table. "Plenty of room for everyone."

I gave him a peering gaze. He ignored it.

Elliott gazed up towards the Knightly Trio – they were still huddled nearby, protectively awaiting any signs of danger. "You three as well. Come and take a seat with us. Join the feast."

Asarra looked confused. "Are you... are you sure, Lord Craven? What if an intruder–"

"This castle, and the island it sits on, is easily defensible on all sides," he reminded them. "It's only tradition that keeps you three so dutifully over there. The purpose for it has long since gone. Hell, if any threat were to appear in this room, it would have already been *inside* the stronghold."

Nikki oddly twitched, but nobody else seemed to notice it. Her eyes met mine with a curious, cat-like smile, but she stayed silent.

Several members of the staff appeared from the kitchen, wielding a wide array of food. To my delight, they cheerfully dropped off what looked like an absolutely *delicious* set of appetizer plates, alongside sharing plates and extra utensils.

"You look particularly happy tonight, more than usual," I told one of the servers.

"Naturally," the butler professionally replied, carrying a sophisticated air of esteem. "It is very rare that we are called upon for a celebration in this castle. We *always* love a reason to party."

"I knew it!" I turned to the vampire lord; he elegantly hid his sly smile behind a glass of blood wine. "What did you tell them?"

"I might have explained the *basic* premise of a birthday party to the staff," he noted dryly.

"*Might* have?"

"Is that what this is?" Lorelei asked aloofly. "I was told something about an important party for our royal guest. Is it your birthday today, then?"

"It is," I answered happily.

"And how old does this make you?"

"Seventeen years old."

She blinked in astonishment. "*Seventeen?* And you're *sentient?* Why, you're no older than a mere child!"

Freezing in place, the serving staff held a wide variety of curious looks on their faces. *Clearly, those guys didn't get the news either...*

"On *our* terms, yes," Elliott noted patiently. "You would be right. However, within the context of humans, Clara is of age."

"Of age for what?" Nikki grinned evilly.

"Of publicly drinking alcohol, at least near an adult," I cut in rather nervously. "Or, of making a ton of incredibly complicated decisions about my future. This is the age where most adults start expecting me to act more like them. I'm definitely not considered a kid anymore, not in a lot of cultures on my world."

"You were a child before today?" Lorelei asked.

"In England, where I'm from? Where we'd be sitting right now, if we were on my Earth? No. I'd be an adult. But across the sea, in another major civilization of my own world, I'd still have to wait one more year for a lot of the things I can do now. I couldn't be around beer, or buy any of the things civilized people consider... obscene."

"Obscene?" Nikki pulled forward in curiosity. "Ooh, *do* tell me more..."

Elliott actually looked slightly embarrassed. "No, that's *quite* enough of that, I think. We aren't here to pick

Clara's brains for the minutiae of her human world, are we?"

"Why *are* we here?" Lorelei asked plainly.

"To celebrate her. We have the first human on our planet in recorded history. Within two weeks of her arrival, she's having a birthday – and unlike the rest of us, with our thousand-year lifetimes, Clara may see less than a hundred. The milestones are far more important to her kind. There are so few of them seen that every one of them counts."

I'd never really thought about the differences in lifespan between Elliott and me. *I mean, yeah, he's a vampire. He's going to live to see **way** more of these than I would...* I turned to him as he quickly educated them on the 'rituals', as he called them. I wasn't listening to the words anymore.

While I grow withered and old, he'll stay frozen in time. Those equinoxes that the vampires have... they put aging on hold. From the deepest reaches of my mind, a small wave of sadness struck me. Now that the thought was there, it infected my mind like a virus.

*Elliott's stuck looking twenty-one or twenty-two, and he'll stay just like that for countless ages... maybe for the entirety of my life, stuck in youth. What would take **me** four or five years might take **him** a century...*

It never really mattered to me before. But now we'd kissed, he and I. We'd confessed a certain level of *feeling* to each other.

Another thought occurred to me. *If you're being suitably honest here... Clara, you haven't discussed what that really means to him, have you?*

What if your aging means differently to him?

That's when the idea first breathed life in the back of my mind. It surprised me that it had never occurred to me before then. But with the insanity of this world and all its intricate similarities to mine, the notion never occurred to me until then...

*Clara – what if you could **become** a vampire?*

Others joined us shortly: Sebastian the sage, and Sabine the sorceress. The two entered together; I noticed them talking in a hushed tone with arms interlocked. The elder vampire leaned in and whispered something in her ear; the sorceress hid a laugh behind her clasped hand.

Those two seem to be getting along, I thought to myself with a smile. *Good. I love seeing people start new friendships.*

"I believe someone mentioned a birthday?" Sebastian greeted us as they approached the table.

"That's right." Nikki's wicked smirk grew into a devious grin, and she pulled me closer with an arm around my shoulder. "Our little human woke up from her coma in time to turn *seventeen*."

"Seven– seven*teen?*" He gasped. "How–"

"Human biology," Elliott quickly answered as the two took their seats, conspicuously beside one another. It was obvious that his patience for giving this explanation had begun to fail him. "No equinoxes, much shorter lifespans. Birthdays are sacred, celebrated events to their culture."

"Well, 'sacred' I'm not so sure about," I leaned in, hoping to spare him from further questions. "But the rest is definitely true. We humans see them as a way to bring friends and loved ones together. A good birthday party is sometimes what it takes to get distant family members in the same room… well, that, or a funeral."

Sabine blinked in confusion, turning to me. "You are so remarkably mature for that age."

"Not really," I grinned as Nikki released her grip on me. "Well, maybe here. But really, I'm no different from any other teenager my age, at least back from where I'm from."

"Forever interesting," the sorceress murmured.

"Come and feast!" Elliott suggested, waving his arm over the spread of food before us. "There are more plates arriving later. For now, I hope you came *hungry*…"

They happily followed his suggestion.

"You know what we need?" Elliott suddenly thought

aloud. "Music. Why don't we have music? This is a party, isn't it?"

"Order for it, then," Lorelei noted quickly.

"I believe I will. Guards?"

A pair of posted guards near an exit to the dining hall dutifully strolled forward. "My Lord?"

"Go down into the tradesman's village within the castle and find us some musicians. A small band will certainly do." He thought for a moment. "I'll sanction one hundred gold apiece, for a couple of hours' work. And tell them that time is of the essence."

"Of course, my Lord."

As they left, Lorelei turned to him. "You could have made it a command. Why pay them?"

"This is a time for celebrating," he smiled. "I want the musicians to reflect that in their music. Why even have them here if they play somberly?" He rested back into his throne. "A better question: what do you think would be a more appropriate guide for the melodies: a command, or a reward?"

A small, reluctant smile slid across her lips.

"Very good, my son. Certainly, you just might make a decent vampire lord after all."

I caught his gaze with wide eyes.

A compliment? From Lorelei?

He clearly felt the same way. Instead of giving a

sarcastic rebuke, Elliott Craven merely lifted his wine glass and smiled into a sip of blood.

***

To describe the rest of the birthday evening, it was nothing short of spectacular. Dinner tasted incredible, and there was far too much food even for our entire party; the musicians were fantastic, and the others in our party kept me laughing with their strange, clashing personalities.

"What are you chuckling about?" Nikki asked curiously as I stifled laughter.

I motioned for her to pull closer.

"It's just, I never realized until tonight just how *badly* that I needed to see Wilhelm and your mum trapped in the same room together."

Nikki watched them with me for a moment.

As usual, Wilhelm was being his typically cheerful and banter-friendly self. Stiffly sitting next to him, composed and statuesque Lorelei valiantly attempted to keep up her normal aloofness.

But the passage of time wasn't being very kind to her patience. The sour, deadpan look quietly growing across her face made us painfully and laughably aware that, even if she was far too proud to admit it, Lorelei was completely and utterly done with being stuck with him.

Nikki bit her lip and stifled laughter.

"Oh my gods, you're completely right."

"Just *look* at her!" I whispered with a grin. "If she has to put up with him any longer, your mum is gonna lose a gasket!"

"A gasket?" Nikki turned. "What's a gasket?"

"Oh, it's a car thing. Like an engine? It, uh..." The look on her face underlined the futility in my explanation. "You know what? Doesn't matter."

We were practically married at the shoulder when Nikki glanced back Lorelei's way. Wilhelm seemed to be miming out some ridiculous bread-baking gesture in his hands towards Viktor, with his head tilted back and his jaw slackened; the former vampire lord, utterly fuming behind her eyes, chose to disappear into a glass of blood.

Asarra merely watched stoically, but I could see a faint smile hidden on her lips.

"What is even going *on* over there?" I asked.

"No idea. Somehow, that makes it better."

Before I could react, there came a commotion from the back. I peered over the mostly destroyed spread of dinner plates towards the back gates.

"Is everything alright?"

Elliott was already rising. "Let me check."

The others gathered gazed at him as he strode down the dining hall towards the kitchen; once he'd passed from sight, the ambient lighting all around us quietly and suspiciously dimmed.

"What is this?" I asked them.

"Beats me!" Wilhelm offered chirpily. "I'm in the dark as much as you are. Get it? In the *dark?*"

"Ugh," Lorelei groaned into her glass.

I couldn't help but laugh. "Oh, don't worry. I thought it was pretty funny."

"You can speak for yourself," Asarra grunted. The way she bit her lip made it tellingly clear she was holding back laughter.

Maybe Wilhelm's got a chance with her after all!

At another clash, our attention was abruptly brought back to the front. There, leading a small procession, marched Elliott Craven with a...

"Oh my God," I covered my face. "You *didn't.*"

"I did," he smiled wickedly, leading a group of servers and kitchen staff. In his confident hands, Elliott proudly held high the most magnificent birthday cake I'd seen, lit ablaze with wax candles. "What good is a birthday without a *cake?*"

I was laughing so hard that I barely heard the vampire lord launch into a rendition of the *Happy Birthday* song... or that everyone at the table, and the serving staff, had apparently been taught the melody as well.

"Haappy birrrthdaay tooo *youuu...*"

"Haappy birrrthdaay *tooo* youuu…"

"Haappy birrrthdaay, dear Claaaraaa…"

As they sang to me, I felt my heart filled with joy. I'd only known these amazing people for two weeks, but that seemed an afterthought to them.

I'd never felt so beloved in my entire life—and it made the terrible events soon after *that much* tougher to bear…

15

CLARA

When the cake was long gone and the festivities wound down, Elliott and I thanked them all for coming out for my birthday.

I hugged everyone as they left – well, *nearly* everyone. Lorelei apparently wasn't having any of that. The former vampire lord stopped me with a cold, mirthless glance before extending her hand. *If that's the best I can get with her standoffishness, then I'll take it.*

Once the others were all gone, Elliott turned to the Knightly Trio with a meaningful grin.

"You three. Take the night off."

"But Lord Elliott," Asarra protested, "we–"

Wilhelm stopped her with his hands on her shoulders. "Let's listen to the master, hmm? If he wants us to take the night off, who's to argue?"

"It is a foolish choice," she muttered. "Why–"

"Come along now, Asarra," Viktor chuckled as he quickly led aside my headstrong guardian. "It's too easy to forget how young you are, my friend. They are reunited. Let the two have their night..."

She cast a searching look my way; honestly, I was mildly terrified with confused eagerness, but Elliott had already clearly gone out of his way to make my seventeenth birthday unforgettable.

"It's okay!" I called after her. "I'll be fine!"

The room cleared, leaving just us. Silence fell over the dining hall for the first time in hours; the anticipation heightened, hanging heavy in the air.

"Have you been enjoying yourself?" He asked.

Oh God, have I not seemed appreciative enough?

"Of course, Elliott! This has been incredible. I couldn't have possibly asked for more."

He took my hand in his.

"Clara, you don't have to ask for anything," he whispered tenderly. "Those days I thought you were ripped away from me, all I could think about was the crushing guilt – guilt over your condition, fear that I'd done that to you."

He looked afraid for a moment, and I palmed his cheek in emotional support. "Elliott... I'm right here. I don't have to go anywhere. We both know I was in great danger here, in this world. What you did probably saved my life."

Since the birthday song, the ambient lighting around us was never changed back to its earlier, brighter levels; we found ourselves still bathed in a dim and romantic glow.

Elliott pressed his forehead to mine. His voice came as a soft murmur in the dark, like a promise threaded through satin. "Everything you want is yours, of all that is within my power to grant."

"You don't have to do that," I whispered.

His husky words replied: "I want to."

We stood like that together, quiet and alone in the dining hall. It felt like eons passed as Elliott and I felt our bond waver between us; this power we shared felt electric in the gap from him to me.

"The servants," I whispered.

"Yes," he nodded. "They'll want to come in to clean the room. We should let them do their work. Perhaps we can find... somewhere else."

"I'd like that," I smiled warmly.

"Good," he smirked. "Come with me..."

"Are you sure about this, Elliott? What if it acts all funny around me?"

"You'll be fine," he insisted playfully.

"I don't know... I'm scared."

"Don't worry. I'll be right here with you."

"O-okay..."

Supportively, Elliott stepped into place at my back. I felt his strong arms envelope my abdomen as we stood together on the chrysm node.

I'd been on one before—with Lorelei, and the Knightly Trio—but only the one. *That was **before** the magical coma...*

The metallic circle under our feet thrummed to life at his touch; red light whirled around us in a column, brightening quickly until it was almost blinding.

"Elliott... Elliott?!"

"Don't worry, Clara!" He laughed happily into my ear, and it sent a small shudder down my skin. "You'll be fine! Just hold on–"

Suddenly, the air crackled around us.

We were suddenly standing in a dark place. Standing on a different node, ours was one out of several in a semi-circle. The overhead lighting shone down much dimmer now, and I could barely see any of my surroundings.

"There," he whispered. "Not so bad, huh?"

"That was..." I shook my head. "Exhilarating! I forget that *that's* what chrysm can do..."

"Chrysm is powerful. It can do many things." He took me by the hand and led me down from the node.

"This is one of its many endless applications. Once my scientists have worked out the technology more, it is my hope that we can bring chrysm travel to the public."

"Oh, that would be wonderful," I gasped as he walked me down a dark hallway. "Do your people have any kind of mass transit?"

"Mass transit?"

"Transportation," I clarified. "Ways of quickly getting from one place to another, perhaps not as *instantaneously* as that..."

"We have livestock for that."

I almost laughed aloud. "I'm *still* trying to get over how weird this is. You live in remote villages and stone castles and you don't have electricity; that makes sense. But you have teleportation and magic indoor lighting, but no phones or Internet? No buses or planes? What kind of wacky priorities do you people have?"

"Our world has different needs than yours," Elliott offered with a deflective shrug. "There are significantly fewer of us, and we live longer lives. We stay within our holds. Traveling to the rival ones can mean certain death to some of us." He clarified: "*Most* of us."

We passed through a large, dim area with an array of gigantic screens attached to an engine far bigger than anything in memory – haphazardly, the screens made some kind of towering wall.

"What is *that?*"

A pair of female workers rushed around a set of complicated instruments and screens beneath the machines. They paused only to look at us, and I felt their inquisitive gazes.

"Your mother didn't take me *here*..."

"She took you on a chrysm trip?" He seemed annoyed.

"Once, yes." His jealousy made me smile. "Only to see her gardens," I quickly added. I tried to not remember the conversation we'd had—where she showed me a stranger, more thoughtful side of herself.

"That explains it. It must have been in Craven Keep. Lorelei keeps one node pair off the network, for whatever reason."

I nodded. "So, tell me about... all of *this,* then."

"This chamber regulates all of the chrysm in Stonehold Castle," he pushed me past. "These two are some of the only attendants in the entire hold who can properly study and control the necessary levels. These machines are far too complicated for many of us to properly maintain; we keep several pairs of these vampires in the castle to run the engines at all times."

Elliott led me down another hallway and to another semi-circular set of chrysm nodes. "Here, Clara... let's take a shortcut to Craven Keep."

"So then, *this* is how you get around the castle so

quickly?" I grinned up at him. "You know what they say about magicians, right?"

"No." He moved me into position on the node. "What do they say?"

"They never reveal their secrets," I shrugged.

"Is that so?" Elliott stepped up onto the node behind me and embraced me from behind. "That's rather sage advice..." I loved how the pressure felt around my stomach.

In fact, I loved the sensation so much that it distracted from the rising, brightening column of red light around us...

<hr />

AFTER THE TELEPORTER BROUGHT US UP TO THE TOP OF Craven Keep, Elliott scooped me into his arms.

I giggled nervously.

Handsome as ever beneath the vivid starlight of another world, the vampire lord brought me back into his private suite. I couldn't read Elliott's intentions... but I could certainly see the ferocity in his eyes; they filled my gut with butterflies.

I hadn't had time to miss Elliott's personal quarters. They were the comfortable place where we'd slept together (well, not like *that*) for the last two weeks.

But after tonight, maybe...

Elliott kicked open the door to his suite as he held me cradled in his strong arms. Neither he nor I uttered a single syllable as he marched us across his contemporary chambers.

When we came to his gothic bedroom, Elliott gently lowered me to his bed.

"Wait here," he smirked slyly. So smitten was I, all I can do was sheepishly nod.

Elliott left me alone for a moment in his dark bedroom; only the hallway lights gave visibility. Brief sounds of activity rumbled in from outside the room until he returned.

"What was that?" I asked.

He descended upon me in an instant, pressing a fingertip against my rosy lips. "Shhh..."

My body rustled with excitement and fear. As his fingertip moved away, replaced with his lips, I felt my chest swell with sensations I'd only barely suffered for other men.

Suddenly, my eyes flared open.

Peter...

In the craziness of the past few weeks, my old crush scarcely flittered through my mind. *Funny to think how absorbed I was with Peter, when the most interesting thing about my daily life was whatever silly bowtie Mr. Collingsworth had chosen to wear for our Sciences class...*

"What's the matter?"

I realized Elliott was watching me quietly.

"Nothing, I just... nothing. Keep going."

He narrowed his eyes suspiciously, but those lips of his lowered to my neck again. A fresh flush of emotion soared across my body, but...

Bitterly, I tried to shove Peter's face out of my head. *That's not fair. I've barely thought about that boy since arriving here. Don't do this to me **now**.* Yet, even after I succeeded, I found that I'd grown less responsive to Elliott's touch.

It's not because of Peter, I groaned.

It's because...

"Clara?"

I sighed. "I'm not ready for this."

He chuckled darkly. "That's fine."

That didn't sound right. "A-Are you sure?"

"Of course I'm sure. If you're not prepared for it, then I'm not going to force it." He lifted his lips back up to mine with a strong, loving kiss. "Clara, I will never make you do anything that you're not comfortable with..."

"Oh God, Elliott," I kissed him back. *Hard.* "I'm so happy to hear that."

He looked amused. "Why?"

"Because plenty of boys on Earth wouldn't tell me anything of the sort. They'd just..." I shivered, thinking of what men on my world were capable of. "They'd take whatever they wanted."

"I am not the *boys* of your world," he smirked.

"No. Of course you're not," I kissed him again. "You're so much better than that."

"Damn right I am."

With those words, we pulled each other into an embrace that lasted halfway until the sun rose again; our limbs intertwined as our lips crashed together all night, again and again...

16

ELLIOTT

Days slipped by, and I felt happier than ever.

Even my times with Silas felt manageable. I'd gladly take a thousand dull, boring counsels with the world's least interesting vampire if it meant Clara was kept out of danger.

But I needn't bother.

From that first night on, it was clear that the spell had ultimately worked after all. For the first time since she'd arrived on the Isle of Obsidian, it seemed clear that Clara Blackwell was safe to walk among my people. The awful bloodlust that consumed all of us was a thing of the past.

My subjects took to her rather quickly, but I'd expect no less. After all, she was creature of myth to them; Clara was the first human being in all of our history to step foot on our world.

Once my royal duties were mostly attended to, she and I began to take walks along the castle grounds. It was a time to get away from our lives and just focus on each other; the opportunity gave us privacy before my responsibilities pulled me back away.

Well, we had *some* privacy. Servant children always ran up to tug at her dress and play with her; it delighted her to see them so happy.

In rare times when I zoned out, my thoughts often wandered back to the things Lorelei told me on the day that Clara woke back up. I wasn't sure that I believed her – but I knew *she* believed them, and that was just as bad.

Her cold, calculated words were soaked in old folklore and ancient stories, long considered false. She spoke of dangers from beyond, of troubles on the horizon, and of a need to visit with mystics and magicians in the wilderness. *Were it anybody else, I'd consider her warnings the rambling stuff of a simple madwoman—but my mother is aloof, not crazy. I have to remember, she's proven me decisively wrong on the topic of* **humans**...

"What are you thinking about, Elliott?"

Curiously watching me, Clara knew that I was lost deep in thought. I snapped my attention back to her with a smile as we rounded a castle hallway together. Nearby, a few of the servants pretended to dust the decorum as they watched her. "Forgive me, Clara. I was just–"

"Thinking to yourself again, yes."

"Have I... have I been doing that a lot, lately?"

She shrugged slyly. "Sometimes."

"You mean, 'all the time.'"

"Yeah," she smiled sadly. "All the time."

I sighed. "Sorry. It's just that I—"

"Have a lot on your mind," she finished for me. Her palm lovingly caressed my cheek. "I get it. I understand. I *know* you have a lot going on. Even after solving the crisis in the mines, there's still a lot of work for you to do..." She nuzzled under my arm, placing a palm to my chest. "Just... try to not lock me out. I can help you. Do you remember what I told you, before we tried that spell?"

So much had happened since then; it was hard to remember. After much pause, I answered: "You said I could use you as a sounding board."

"That's right. I still mean it. Get some of that stuff out of your head." She affectionately poked the side of my skull. "Can't stay up there forever."

My thoughts scattered.

*Do I tell her? Silas warned me only this morning. There's no time for me to prepare; of course, that's exactly how **they** want it. But I can lean on Nikki for advice. Perhaps even Lorelei might be of some service this time, as doubtful as that—*

"Elliott," she murmured, her fingertips lightly

running down my forearm. "You're doing it again, you silly vampire. You're locking me out."

I sighed. "It's the vampire lords."

"Oh?" She paused attentively. "What now?"

I thought back to when Akachi Azuzi entered the castle, searching for her. His appearance was a formality, but he'd confirmed she was there. He'd *felt* her, just like Lorelei and I had when Clara first arrived in our castle out of thin air. That was the moment that pushed me to have the protection spell performed on her; as a result, I almost lost her forever.

"It seems the others have called a council," I replied grimly. "The rulers of the Eight Holds are all expected to meet, and I can only imagine what they want to discuss..."

"Me," she groaned.

"If I'm wrong, I'll eat the entire throne myself." With a snarl, I slammed my fist into the marble wall; a servant jumped, and a few hairline cracks splintered across the stone. "I've only just gotten you back, safe and sound. I *refuse* to let them try and take you away from me."

"They can *try*," she looped her arm through mine. "But I know you'll never let them."

I sighed. Honestly, from the very instant that I first laid my eyes on Clara Blackwell, I'd known that this was coming, and I'd dreaded it all the while. *The only reason I have any claim to her is that she appeared in **my** castle, and they* *all know it. I'm the youngest and least senior among them... there's no way in hell that the others will allow me to keep her for long, not without a fight...*

"Elliott..."

"I know," I growled a little harder than I meant to. "I just don't know what to do."

"Yes you do," she reassured me.

It's true, I grunted bitterly to myself. There was no escaping the truth, no matter how much I wanted to. *I do know what to do. Not that I **like** it, especially knowing how they are...*

"I have to meet with them," I conceded.

"You do. And you have to win them over."

My gaze averted. "I don't know that I can."

Clara's lips sought mine as she pulled me into a loving embrace. "I *know* you can," she whispered to me in a hushed voice. "I believe in you, Elliott Craven. You're capable of such great things. With time, this will be just another example of what you can truly accomplish."

I planted a kiss on her forehead.

*I hope you're right, for **both** our sakes...*

※

ONCE I LEFT CLARA IN THE CARE OF HER LOYAL guardians, I turned my attention towards the medical bay.

Out of the five, Kinsey was the only one of the guards from that day who was awake at the time. Sometimes it was one of the others instead; they seemed to rest in shifts, as if their bodies operated in terms of the royal guards even as they healed.

"Lord Elliott," she looked up at me. "Welcome back. How is the world out there?"

"Difficult as always," I answered dejectedly as I pulled up a seat. "How would you like to be left in control of the hold? I'll switch places with you. *You* can deal with the other vampire lords, and *I'll* laze about with a nurse tending to every whim all bloody day."

"That bad, huh?"

I lowered my head. "Dreadful."

The guard didn't respond. I lifted up my head again to see that Kinsey sat upright, staring at me.

"You know, my Lord... you don't *have* to come check on us like this. We have our own superiors who swing by every day for progress reports."

"My life is safe, thanks to you lot."

Her face told me she didn't accept the answer. "You sent us back up to the surface without you, my Lord, while you defeated the creature alone. If anything, *you* saved *our* lives."

"One of your count died protecting me. The rest of you lie here, grievously wounded after you did the very same. I do not so easily forget those who lay their lives down on the line for mine. I know it's your sworn duty, but that doesn't make the order any easier—and yet, none of you complained for an instant. You ascended to the challenge and fought with me against incredible odds."

"I would do it again in an instant."

"That, I do not doubt," I smirked. "But I want you to know that I meant what I told you in that cave, when we were the only two awake after the beast's attack."

"Which was what?"

She coughed before I could answer; I held a glass of water for her and sadly averted my gaze. "I'll never lead you into such danger like that again. Not blindly."

I lowered the glass when she finished sipping.

"You know, with what you said earlier... you were right, Lord Craven. It *is* our sworn duty to protect. There is no higher honour than to serve you, whether to live in glory or die trying. So long as it means you get to rule the hold another day, any of us would die to defend your life."

"You were admirable at it."

"That's the highest praise I could hope for."

"No, there's higher," I observed. "The others, they all fought valiantly in the line of duty. But the rest, while all quite talented on their own right, lack your mettle and your compassion. They are also healing at a *significantly* worse rate than you..."

"Always been a little lucky," she shrugged.

"Today continues the trend," I replied, smiling smugly. "Sadly, your companions here will be worse for wear for surviving the encounter with the tatzelwurm. On the other hand, Kinsey, you are expected to make a full recovery..."

"That's good news."

"...Which is why, once you've healed, I plan to make you my vassal. Do you accept?"

"Your vassal?"

"I've spoken with the sage; he enlightened me to the details. It is a ceremonial way for a vampire lord to choose specific bodyguards. As a bonus, the ritual elevates those of particular merit to the Court of Stonehold. You will be a proper knight."

"You want me to bodyguard you?"

"Can't think of a more appropriate guard. At my side, you helped me face down one of the most horrific beasts we've seen. Were any of the others going to be in suitable physical condition, I'd extend the same hand to them... but it appears that you are the only guard from that day to come back just as strong as ever." I leaned towards her. "Kinsey, become my vassal. Serve a permanent post at my side—for the duration of my reign."

"Thank you, Lord Elliott. I... I just don't know what to say." She glanced away.

"Think on it," I told her, pulling myself up out of my

chair. "I expect to be distracted for the next few days, so you'll have time."

Had I only known how 'distracted' I'd really be. My eyes stayed firmly set on the threat of the vampire lords, but danger lurked just around the nearest corner. My entire life was about to be thrown into complete and utter disarray, because the most immediate threat was a *whole* lot closer than I could have possibly realized...

17

SABINE

A dark new dawn rose over Stonehold Castle.

From my vantage point high along the castle walls, the Isle of Obsidian was freshly awash with the morning glow. It turned the island into an ethereal sight under our supernatural skies.

Memorize this, Sabine, for it's the final day that you'll see this view...

In the three days since making my decision, I came here during the sunrises to remember just how beautiful this all looked. It was the one thing I knew I'd miss about my time here, so close to the vampire lord of Stonehold.

I had played a dangerous game, coming here. Years of planning went into positioning myself to come here, awaiting the right chance and just the proper timing...

Once I'd slipped into the inner circle of Elliott Craven, I had expected a clear path forward.

*Yet, you found opportunities for bigger things, didn't you? After all this, the only thing you weren't prepared for was the allure of a **bigger** prize...*

As if on cue, she was beside me.

"You're up early," I noticed.

Nikki Craven stifled a yawn as she crawled up onto the battlement at my side.

"I truly do not understand why you insist on sitting in such blatantly *dangerous* spots," my head shook in utter disbelief. "You are bound to seriously injure yourself, one of these days..."

"Aw," the deranged vampire twisted her face towards me. "Does Sabine *care* about little old me? Does she *care* for my safety?"

I crossed my arms. "Don't be foolish."

"Nah," she chuckled darkly. "Of course not."

Nikki slid over sideways; for a moment, I was afraid that the maniac was going to plummet off the side of the stronghold. *Even vampire lord blood won't hold up to **that**!* But then I could see that she was dangling upside-down, grinning madly from the flattened tooth of the castle wall.

"Come back up from there," I ordered.

"No," she winked. "I like it like this."

"All the blood will rush to your head."

"I do my best thinking like that."

"No you don't."

She grinned wickedly. "Nah, you're right."

Even after our few days of covertly meeting, I wasn't entirely sure what to make of my new ally. Nikki Craven was a wildcard, but then there were the things that she'd told me of the other holds...

Elliott is a fool to not use her, I noted.

*So perhaps **I** will...*

"Have you decided yet?" She asked, bored.

Gravely, I crossed my arms. "Yes."

Nikki swung from her upside-down position to grasp between the battlements in front of me. Effortlessly holding herself by her fingers as she dangled from the castle wall, she supplied a prime example of a vampire lord's strength. *Even if she is not the reigning lord, Elliott's death would mean the hold would become **hers**...*

What a terrifying thought.

"So?" She giggled. "What did you choose?"

With a sigh, I glanced up at the dawning sun again. Its light bathed the island in such beauty; it made me wonder if I should reconsider after all.

Life here is unusual, I thought to myself. *Elliott Craven just might make a reasonable ruler yet. At this point, he requires suitable advisors. If he lets the right ones in, they could help him continue the work of his predecessor—and build a prosperous era for Stonehold...*

I could stay, I remembered. *I could remain here and leave him none the wiser—and abandon all my former plans. My true allegiance could remain here instead; it wouldn't really be all **that** difficult to simply become a servant to the Cravens...*

"I've opted to change my mind," I told Nikki.

"Oh?" She lifted herself up to peacefully leer at me in her own twisted way. "So, you've decided to give up on your plan for the moment?"

"I wouldn't quite say that."

She tilted her head. "Out with it, Sabine."

My eyebrow arched. "*Change* of plans, is all."

The insane vampire grinned toothily as she swayed her dangling torso back and forth, down out of sight, patiently awaiting more.

"I am going to take Clara Blackwell."

Nothing about her movements changed; even her eyes seemed just the same. The swaying of the vampire's body below her shoulders didn't shift even an inch. Yet, the powerful intuition that had guided me this far was giving me a peculiar feeling about the younger Craven, all of a sudden. It was some small and imperceptible change.

Something feels... different.

"Can I still count on your help, Nikki?"

She smirked evilly. "What kind of ally would I be if I declined? I'm a little miffed you chose to change things up on me, but..." Nikki lunged up from the battlement and gracefully landed on the opposite one behind me in a crouch. "Change, like many things in this world, is *meant to hurt*..."

"Why? Do you like things to hurt, Nikki?"

The demented vampire grinned. "Always."

I couldn't help stifling laughter. "Well, that's certainly good to hear. I have great need of you to administer a little... pain. You will need to subdue Clara if we have any hope of getting her out of the castle undetected."

"Subdue?" She licked her lips evilly. "I feel like I can manage 'subdue'..." Her head tilted again as she squinted her eyes. "But when do you plan for this to happen?"

"As I understand it, your brother leaves today to meet with the other vampire lords."

Nikki's eyes widened. "You meant *today?*"

"Yes, why? Is that a problem?"

"Well, it's just that the chrysm..."

The crouching lunatic paused, her eyes on me with cat-like cunning; if it weren't for her sick and demented mind, I'd have thought Nikki Craven was *plotting*...

With a blink, that side of her was gone. *Maybe she was dueling with sanity,* I chuckled inwardly.

"Another day," she daintily shook her head, as if she were clearing it. "Must've been thinking of another day... funny, how often I can get them so *very* mixed up."

Something doesn't seem right....

"Nikki, are you *certain* you're up for this?"

"For harming Clara Blackwell? Ever since that little

human brat wound up here, it's caused my brother *boundless* trouble. Maybe he's a tad better off without her as a... distraction..."

That lacked her usual malice.

"You don't sound convincing."

Nikki's eyes glinted with a devilish gleam. "It doesn't matter if you think I am or not. The things in my head that I fight on a daily basis *crave* blood and carnage..." She crept down from the stones in a truly terrifying crawl, rising up before me. Every story that I'd ever heard of the dreaded warrior of the wilds—a bloodthirsty combatant wandering from settlement to settlement, hunting only the deadliest creatures of the land and upending countless mercenary guilds—seemed suddenly very true. So few of the common-folk knew what the Cravens looked like, and had thus worked out that *that* creature and Princess Nikki Craven were one and the same—and before me rose the terrifying amalgamation of the two entities.

"Feed me something to torment, and I will."

Either Nikki Craven is the world's best actress, I laughed with equal parts shock and approval, *or she is **definitely** on my side after all...*

"So, shall we plan?" She tilted her head.

"Yes," I grinned. "Yes, we shall..."

18

ELLIOTT

Down within the teleportation hub, I walked up towards the vertical tower of massive monitors. Incomprehensible charts, graphs, and figure sets flickered across screens almost as tall as I was.

Micromanaging all the various chrysm levels of Stonehold Castle, the pair of female attendants barely noticed me approach. Their nimble fingers flew across keyboards as they kept their eyes on the gigantic screens, studying a ridiculous density of information.

It was far beyond my capacity to understand, so I left them to their devices. Instead, I walked the short breadth of the hub atrium, ignoring the five hallways that stretched towards the various clusters of teleportation nodes.

My destination was far more interesting.

Around the side of the pillar of machines and screens stood a simple panel door, obscured by the atrium's darkness. I pushed through the easily overlookable entrance to reveal a staircase, rising up into the hidden chamber of the chrysm hub.

The stairs lit up at my presence, one at a time. The rising illumination revealed rolling fog that drifted down the stairs – a natural byproduct of the chrysm ore's cooling systems.

It never brought me joy to come here.

Solemnly, I ascended towards the single most important teleportation node in the castle. There were only about a dozen steps, but each one filled me with rising dread.

I stepped onto the tiled glass platform.

It always filled me with awe to see this device. After all, this was no mere teleportation node...

The portal stood powerfully before me, glowing with unrestrained might. Tall enough to fit Clara standing on my shoulders, it commanded total respect. This was the most vital defense point of not only *this* castle, but of *every* castle. Every hold in the world had a portal just like this one in their castle somewhere, ready to send their vampire lords to any connected part of the realm that they saw fit to visit.

Nodes were two-way closed circuits.

Portals, however... well, they could blink you *anywhere*

in the entire global portal network. And that included any other castle on the planet...

Long-range chrysm teleportation required far more power to properly control. This entire room was designed to keep the highly volatile ore at the coolest temperature available. As such, the glass beneath my boots was incredibly thick. It was even coated on the underside with a transparent, heatproof layer, protecting it from melting in the intensity of the castle's chrysm ore reservoir.

Two feet of solid glass separated me from a cruel fate of boiling alive in what was effectively a small, highly volatile volcano of magical magma.

The gatekeeper stood quietly before me. To resist the effects of ongoing chrysm radiation, her head was fitted with a special plate visor. This meant that her face was completely shielded with segmented plates of thinly hammered steel – just like her plated gloves, which were instrumental in her work. The plates were all designed to not only shift comfortably with her motions, but to deflect most of the side effects of single-handedly guarding the castle's most vulnerable entry point.

The gatekeeper bowed her head respectfully. "Greetings, Lord Craven." She gestured towards the portal. "Do you wish to leave the castle?"

"Yes," I answered reluctantly.

Dramatically holding out a plated glove, the gatekeeper turned towards the monolithic portal and wove her fingers expertly through the air.

"Lord Craven, where would you like to go?"

Crossing my arms defiantly, I summoned up every last drop of remaining courage. Mentally, I prepared myself for the viper's nest I was about to voluntarily descend into.

"Take me to the Council of the Eight Holds."

THE COUNCIL CHAMBER'S TRUE LOCATION WAS A TOTAL mystery, to even all of us vampire lords. Lorelei was one of the last to know the true location, as her chrysm revolution had brought this place to be. She told no one—not even I.

Shrouded in secrecy, the chamber acted as the single connecting point of all the holds on Earth. It was here alone that the vampire lords convened to discuss matters affecting the entire realm.

It was also where we turned on one another.

In a desolate chamber bathed in complete darkness, I stepped out from a special node. The surfaces of this room were rough and unrefined, from a great many centuries before we designed more efficient architectural techniques.

The only worthwhile feature was a primitive doorway

in front. Dusky light lazily filtered from down the hallway; I followed a barren and lifeless path that had been long ago whittled out of solid, flawless rock. *Seems the creators had quite the lingering fascination for chilling, soulless design...*

My gaze trailed up to the ceiling. Natural light came in from outside of these passageways, but there was no way these were built outside. I could almost hear the creaking and rumbling of distant, earthy noises; it was like listening to the breaths of the very earth around me.

When I had asked Lorelei about the light, she'd merely scoffed. It seemed that nobody knew how the paths were lit with trailing, dusty light, or how the chrysm teleporter node was supported without any nearby supply.

After a few moments of walking the trail, never rising nor falling, an empty doorway carved into the stone awaited me.

With a deep breath, I stepped through the gate and into the real Council of the Eight Holds. *Time to face off against the other vampire lords—for the fate of Clara Blackwell's life.*

19

CLARA

To keep my mind off of Elliott's meeting with the vampire lords, I descended back into the hobby I'd enjoyed before all the magical nonsense.

Reading.

While I comfortably holed up within Elliott's suite, the Knightly Trio decided to let me focus on my book. When I found their trance thing to be a little too distracting, I asked them if they'd let me read it alone.

Asarra wasn't pleased to hear it. "Are you sure that is such a good idea? I do not like this."

"It'll be fine!" I grinned.

"But... Lord Elliott–"

"Lives in a stronghold with no way inside or out that doesn't go through the defenses," I tried to reassure her.

"He said it himself at my birthday party, remember? You'll be right here, it's just that, well..."

"What, is it creepy?" Viktor asked.

"Uh, it *can* be, sometimes."

Wilhelm chuckled. "Well, fine then. If you're so utterly dead-set on it, I suppose Craven Keep *is* the most fortified part of the castle. It's not like we aren't, oh, I don't know, standing near the top of one of the toughest towers in the whole world..."

"I'm not sure," Asarra groaned. "Lord Elliott—"

"Isn't here," I smiled sympathetically. "When he made you three my guardians, he asked you to do whatever I asked of you, right?"

The knight opened her mouth to respond.

"*Within reason,*" I quickly added.

"I... yes, that is true."

"Wilhelm said it himself: this tower is highly fortified. Nobody's getting in or out of here unless they go through you, right?"

The three of them shared a look, but I knew I had already won the argument.

"Sounds good to me!" Wilhelm grinned.

Viktor frowned. "I, uh... well... okay."

"Fine." Asarra groaned in defeat, grumpily lowering her head. "We will wait out on the stairs for you to read some of your book..."

"Thanks!" I grinned. "You won't regret it."

After I watched them settle outside, I closed the door and made myself comfortable in a chair. Tucked away with the hardback book that I had been reading in the days leading up to my coma, I nestled into the cushions and found my place in the pages again.

My fingers absentmindedly fiddled with the black necklace around my neck; something buried deep down in my mind told me I needed to keep it a secret from everyone, so I did.

It had belonged to my grandmother. That's all that I could really remember about it, but it felt like something of...

It was hard to entertain the thought.

But it felt like a relic of *power*.

Still, I had no answers as to how it wound up around my neck again, but I *did* have a book to read... and so, I descended into the stories again.

Had I been a little older and wiser, I would've just listened to Asarra – because they *did* regret it. I should have never let them leave the room. We *all* regretted that choice in the long hours that soon followed. My naivete and foolishness set into motion powerful events that would change *everything* forever.

Because, the truth of the matter was that I'd just made the biggest mistake of my life.

Destiny came in the form of a distracting noise.

I glanced up from the book. "What was that?"

Nothing answered. For a moment, I thought I heard some kind of commotion outside the door, like a few faint buzzing sounds and then a hard, heavy thud. But the moment that I'd looked away from the novel in my hands, it was gone.

Well. That's certainly odd.

"Elliott?"

Nothing changed.

My face twisted with a frown. *This thing with the vampire lords has me on edge,* I reasoned. *After all, Elliott made it super clear that they could put me in serious danger...*

Yeah, I nodded to myself. *That must be it.*

Eager to shake off the ominous feeling about the dangers of faraway vampire royalty, I turned my attention back to the book. It had just started getting really good again; I eagerly wanted to see where it would take me.

Besides, I reminded myself, *the Knightly Trio is still out there. They were fully trained royal guards. If something were to happen, they could handle it.*

The door clicked open.

"Wilhelm, if that's you, then I..."

As I glanced up at the sight in the doorway, my words meaninglessly trailed off into the air. Judging by the motionless bodies draped against the stairs, there wasn't anybody coming to save me this time.

The hardback clattered to the floor as I leapt up from the chair. "No..." In my growing terror, the word was barely higher than a whisper.

Before I could try and scream for help, the vampire murderously descended upon me.

Everything soon went black.

20

ELLIOTT

Within the small and circular room, carved out deep within the ground somewhere on Earth, the Council of the Eight Holds awaited me.

Every hold ruler had his or her own throne; together, they all formed a central ring of power. Each throne sat firmly in its own half-quadrant, divided from its peers by ancient magical shields and clearly meant to keep us from tearing one another apart. I could only imagine what kind of political bloodshed must have occurred in the old days to require such precautions...

Despite arriving ten minutes early, I was still the last of us to appear within the council chamber. The others were speaking in hushed tones as I stepped into the room; they quieted as I took my seat.

Akachi Azuzi turned to me, stroking his long and elderly beard. "Greetings, Lord Craven..."

I gave him a curt nod. Despite our animosity, I was better served by feigning politeness than picking a fight with him in front of the others.

*With so much at stake... that goes **double**.*

"It is good to see you again so soon, after our little visit," Azuzi mused aloud for the group's benefit. *So, they already know. No possibility for me to spring that as an accusatory surprise, then...* "Tell me, how are things in Stonehold? I hear that there's been some trouble in the mines?"

"Things have been settling for the better," I responded tersely. "It's true, chrysm mining has taken a few hits in the passing months. But I've been assured that the worst's already behind us."

"Is that so? Good," he smiled curtly. "I would hate for your hold's supply to run out. With the amount of it we rely on, that could certainly cause some alarm among the rest of us..."

I couldn't tell if he knew more, or was merely trying to psyche me out before the council. *Either way, I won't give him the satisfaction...*

The vampire lord of Bleakwood rose from his throne. Tall, broad-shouldered Mattias Blackburn reigned over a frozen region of desolate tundra and gnarled, haunted forests far across the ocean.

If we had a leader—and we didn't—he would be the closest thing to it. No vampire lord dared to defy him; in return, the ruler of Bleakwood was *very* particular when he rarely voicing his opinion. "I hereby call into session the Council of the Eight Holds," he spoke in his booming voice. "We have all been called together today to address an exceptionally *interesting* rumour..."

Mattias quietly lowered his gaze onto me.

"Allegedly, a human has come to Earth."

The others turned. The collective strength of their curious stares underlined an intimidating point: I had the undivided attention of the seven most influential vampires in the world...

Mattias stoically asked: "Anything to add?"

I could try to deny it, but there was no telling what rumours had already spread to their holds.

*This is a game that I must play **very** carefully...*

My fingers curled around the armrests of my throne, whitening my knuckles. "It's true. There is a human on our world."

Hushed mutters spread among the others.

"*Silence, my Lords!*" Mattias ordered. "You can mindlessly speculate to your hearts' content *after* we learn more of this... most unexpected visitor."

I didn't trust him any more than the others, but there was no denying his prevailing voice of reason and sensible air. These qualities had given me a begrudging respect for Lord Blackburn.

"Continue, Lord Craven."

Drifting my gaze around the ring of thrones, I took a moment to briefly study their expressions. They hid their true intentions well. If this were a high-stakes game for the fate of the world, I'd be at a complete loss. *But Elliott,* I considered: *in a lot of ways, isn't that **exactly** what this is?*

"Just over two weeks ago, I felt the presence of an intruder in Stonehold Castle."

"*Felt?*" Svetlana Lovrić smirked in a casual air. Equally enigmatic and beautiful, the ruler of the nearby Drenchlands lifted a questioning eyebrow. "What is this, 'felt' you speak of?"

"Something felt wrong," I explained carefully. "Lorelei Craven sensed it too. We sensed the arrival of a mysterious guest that didn't belong. My guards found her first. They brought her to me."

"So it *is* a 'her'," Mattias noted calmly.

I shouldn't have been surprised they already knew that. Instead of annoyance, I redirected my irritation into relief that I'd made the right choice in being forthright.

If I had lied to them, I'd have lost any semblance of control in this meeting...

"Yes. The human is a woman."

"A woman?" Eyes-Like-Fire shook her shaved and

bone-pierced head. Her striking appearance was dominated with the traditional tribal tattoos of her nomads, a proud and mystical vampire people. "I heard that she was a *girl*..."

"Their lifespans are much different than ours," I replied nonchalantly. "In the context of a human lifetime, she says that she's already–"

"She *says?*" Akachi asked suddenly.

"Yes," I responded tensely, not understanding.

Lord Blackburn turned to me. "Before I form an opinion on these affairs, I wonder: how similar to vampires *is* this human, Lord Craven?"

"I don't think I understand."

He hid a small smile. "Does she think?"

I realized now what Akachi meant.

"Does she *think?*" I blinked in total surprise. "*Of course* she thinks! We're not discussing some stray animal here —the human almost passes for one of our kind. She even speaks our language and reads our books." I crossed my arms in defiance. "Does she *think*...? Lord Blackburn, you insult her intelligence."

The rest of the room pondered this; in fleeting realization, it occurred to me that I might have given away too much about her. But the thought of them lumping Clara into the same category as a common animal angered me.

"You were saying something about lifespans," Mattias

noted again. "That they are different than ours? Care to elaborate?"

"Humans do not have the equinoxes that we enjoy. As they continuously age, their lifespans are significantly shorter than those of vampires," I reluctantly admitted while thinking of how to leverage this information. *Perhaps I can convince them to think of her less as a naive girl, and more of an intelligent and thoughtful woman...* "She may be young, but the girl tells me that she's lived nearly the first *fifth* of her years."

"A fifth?" Svetlana Lovrić scoffed. "How long is a human life, if she is but a girl?"

Begrudgingly, I answered: "Eighty years to a century, under the right conditions."

The vampire lords burst into a loud flurry of loud derision and laughter. "Under a *century?*" Lord Lovrić heartily laughed, wiping at her eye. "Why, they're nothing but *children!*"

During their brief distraction, I tried to quietly rehearse a way of taking control of the conversation. *I can't let the rest force me to stay on the defense. I'll be boxed into a corner over her...*

I felt eyes on me, and I turned.

With his fist clasped hard in his hand, elbows propped on the armrests of his throne, I realized that Mattias Blackburn was quietly watching me. *What I wouldn't give to have that extrasensory perception right this moment...*

Akachi Azuzi grinned wickedly, taking the opportunity to address me. "Seems to me that our little Lord Craven has made himself *quite* the scholar to the ways of humankind..."

I didn't like his smug comment. Particularly, I didn't like how it met thoughtful stares and quiet murmurs of agreement. But in this game of chess, I could see no appropriate answer... so I allowed my questioning glare to do the talking for me.

"Tell me, my Lord," Akachi narrowed his eyes. "Why is it that you chose against convening the Council of Eight Holds yourself? Given all the flying rumours, you should have *known* we would listen..."

The room went silent at the accusation.

"She has not been here long," I replied. "I had to be certain that I wasn't wasting your time, and that included conferring with Lorelei Craven..." I hated to hide behind her name, but I needed any shield I could find. "You pre-empted me by only a couple of days. After all, there was no guarantee that the human wouldn't vanish, just as quickly as she arrived..."

"So, you did not summon her here?" Svetlana tilted her head curiously. "I was told that you had found a way to pull humans to Earth."

"Seriously?" I had to stifle incredulous snickering. "Go back and ask me three weeks ago if humans existed; I'd have laughed in your face. In fact, I *almost* did just that, when my sage himself first brought up the suggestion."

I chuckled in perplexed amusement. "No, my dear Lord—I am no miracle worker. I haven't quite discovered how to summon mythical creatures from beyond the veil into our own world, nor did I ever *believe* in them..."

Most of the others snickered or laughed too; Sveltana looked embarrassed. It was good for my case to have finally gotten some of them to smile.

Akachi looked unperturbed. "Your reasoning makes sense enough, Lord Craven, but here is the real question... when do you plan to bring the human before us? Surely, you don't wish to hoard such a historic visitor all to *yourself*..."

I should have seen it coming. He'd backed me into a corner, and we both knew it. I had no choice but to rely on the truth – or some version of it.

"You'll all try to drink her to death before you even get the chance," I replied gravely. "The tales are true about human blood. The very scent of it triggers a powerful bloodlust, especially when it comes to vampire lords."

"Haven't already drunk her bone-dry, then?" Akachi cruelly spoke. "Such persevering restraint you must have... after all this time, I have clearly underestimated you."

"I had a spell cast on her," I noted.

"Oh. Well, problem solved!"

I leaned forward. "It didn't *entirely* work," I explained, lying through my teeth.

"Get a better magician, then!" Akachi grinned. "In fact, for an hour alone with the girl, I'll even lend you one of mine! Just to talk, of course..."

"Of course," I narrowed my eyes.

Mattias spoke up. "Lord Craven, what caused the spell to fail?"

I considered my words carefully.

"Without another human to confirm, there's no telling. It's either because of *her* in particular, or humans are naturally resistant to magic."

The room went dead quiet.

"What exactly are you saying, Lord Craven?" Valentine Vasiliev, ruler of The Wastes, spoke in thin accusation. The cold and calculating vampire lord leaned forward in a dark, foreboding tone. "'Resistant to magic?' *Nobody* and *nothing* on this planet is 'resistant to magic', Lord Craven..."

"Yet, human beings are a *fairy tale*, nothing more than folklore we tell to young vampires." I tilted my head authoritatively. "Whether or not you believe me, and I'd honestly rather you didn't, I'm telling you that a human is in Stonehold. And magic doesn't *quite* take to her."

"We believe you," Eyes-Like-Fire rolled a bone piercing in her ear between her playful fingers. "We all felt the human arrive."

Wait.

WHAT.

Mattias Blackburn turned to me. "We all knew she was here, Lord Craven. Every vampire lord on Earth felt her appear on Earth. The only problem is that we didn't know *where* she was..."

I sank back into my seat.

It had never occurred to me that they'd feel her arrival as well. The sensation must have been limited in scope, but if this was true... if they'd *all* known as soon as I did...

Then I'd been screwed from the start.

Certainly explains how the rumours travelled so quickly...

"Cheer up, Lord Craven," Akachi Azuzi smiled over at me. "With that look on your face, it sounds like you just found out your mother died."

The others turned on him angrily for daring to make that joke, but I barely heard any of them. Clara was in much greater danger than I thought. The grim reality of the situation had been made ten times worse than my deepest, darkest fears...

"Order!" Mattias bellowed. "Order, all of you!"

There was no way to play this safe anymore. If they'd known all along that Clara was on Earth, and they'd now confirmed that she was in my hold, then the only way to keep her protected was to go off the rails. *It's time to show them who I am.*

My gaze lifted as I sat forward.

"What are your plans for the girl?"

The others looked at each other.

"Plans?" Eyes-Like-Fire asked confusedly.

"There's no telling when she might vanish," I told them in no uncertain terms. "She might even be gone by the time I return. But if I were to bring her here, what would you want? How can we best utilize this gift?"

Mattias leaned forward. "Just to be clear, Lord Craven, are you suggesting that you'd be willing to part with the human?"

I ignored the question.

"Let us dispense with the formalities." My gaze drifted around the ring. "All of you have already thought up some plan or another. Some, far more obvious than others..." Before moving on, I briefly lingered on Akachi's cold stare. "Feel free to lay all your cards on the table, all of you. This is a place for discussion. If I can be convinced that there is a plan that mutually benefits us *all*, and it keeps the human traveler safe, then I'm open to debate."

The vampire lords remained silent. Fleeting glances

among them told me that half of them waited to see if any others would speak up.

"If *any* of you choose to attack Stonehold, you will plunge the world into war. I won't hesitate to defend my people, or guests of my royal family, and just to make it painfully apparent: the human is the guest of the Cravens. Striking at Stonehold will not shatter my resolve. There is too much at stake now, and we understand so very little. All I ask is, if you do not present a better idea... allow me to discover what I can." I smiled sincerely. "In return, I will share all that I learn."

Akachi Azuzi narrowed his eyes menacingly. "A nice speech, but you forget something, little Lord Craven: she is not your right. You *will* bring the human to us or suffer the consequences. Do we make ourselves clear?"

I rose from my throne to glare down at him. "*You?* Yes. But you are *one* among *many*. Tell me, my Lords..." I glanced around the thrones. "Are the rest of you so willing to risk global warfare to secure your ownership of this single human girl? One, might I remind you, who travels between worlds by *complete accident?*"

Confronting the room, I held my arms up in authority. "Let us not play pretend: warfare will throw my hold *and yours* back half a millennium of prosperity. Maybe even more. And while Lord Azuzi seems so very willing to jeopardize your main source of chrysm development and mining by threatening Stonehold, I can't help but find myself wondering if you share his..." I met his glare with my own. "...Enthusiasm."

I sat down, leaning back into my throne. "My Lords, what I suppose you must ask yourselves, is... well, is it worth the cost?"

The vampire lords carefully studied me with various expressions. Nearly all of them showed me some form of approval, amusement, or quiet envy. Only Akachi seemed to hold a furious glare.

"There doesn't appear to be any clear dissent," Mattias Blackburn observed. "Then, for now, I see no reason for us to interfere with the human's life. But rest assured, Lord Craven..." He leaned forward with a bold, imposing stare. "You will be asked to bring her forward for questioning... or *made* to, should it be necessary."

As I met his gaze with a respectful nod, I found it hard to revel in my fleeting victory. That is, not with the collective attention of the world's leaders, all turning to me again menacingly...

21

ELLIOTT

Preoccupied with wrath, I barely acknowledged the gatekeeper as I descended the stairs.

The vampire lords and their unspoken threats would have to wait. It was far more pertinent that I rally with Nikki – she'd been conspicuously hard to find in the castle today. I'd given up and just had to visit the council before we could confer.

When I pushed out into the atrium, my boots took me straight towards the proper hallway. My steady strides turned to a run as I dove down the dim passageway to the round platform of raised node clusters, stepping onto the second from the left and waiting for the teleportation to activate.

Seconds passed.

When the chrysm didn't flare, I was honestly taken

aback. I stepped off of the node and tried it again. Nothing happened.

Irrational panic grasped at my throat. I could feel it – something was wrong, and it wasn't *just* with the malfunctioning node...

Furiously, I stalked my way back into the main atrium and clasped my hand on the closest attendant's shoulder.

"What is the matter? The node to Craven Keep isn't functioning."

She didn't flinch, keeping herself busy with her work. "Lord Craven, we sent those details to you *days* ago. Eighteen of twenty-five transporter nodes – including the one to Craven Keep – were marked for full deactivation today. We anticipate several hours of chrysm maintenance."

My jaw dropped. *EIGHTEEN? But that's almost the entire teleportation array!* There wasn't time for arguing this; I quickly composed myself.

"When did this start?"

The attendant briefly glanced at a clock. "The system is offline, effective one hour ago."

"Why am I only hearing of this *now?*"

Without skipping a beat, the other attendant shrugged. "Silas made it clear that he'd tell you. If he hasn't, then that's a tremendous breach in the chain. We can't have the royal family unaware of temporary breakdowns in major transportation. Both of the Ladies

Craven have confirmed debriefing... were you, my Lord, not informed at all of the scheduled repairs?"

I was beside myself with fury, but I couldn't blame the high chancellor for this one. *Half the time, I don't even bother listening to him,* I reminded myself bleakly. *There's no way that I can confirm he hasn't mentioned this to me...*

"Shall I file a revocation order for Silas?"

"No," I shook my head. "Forget him. I have to reach my private quarters *now*. If the castle only has *seven* operational teleports... which one of my chrysm nodes will get me the closest?"

They shared a brief glance before returning to their workflow. "Second chamber, center node."

I turned and bolted for the appropriate spot. Once reaching the node, I hopped on the circular platform and waited for the familiar column of red, brightening light to slowly overwhelm me...

The teleportation hub vanished from sight.

Instead, I was standing in a hidden closet, built specifically for the purpose of moving across the castle undetected. I pushed my way out, raced down a hallway, made a turn, another turn, and pushed out through the large gates...

No, I gasped.

I stood at the edge of the bailey, staring nearly halfway across the castle at Craven Keep.

Dropping to a knee in the dirt, I ignored the peculiar

looks I earned from passing servants and tradesmen. Pressing my fingertips down into the moist ground in front, I focused on my breathing and coiled my muscles...

With a sudden dash, I burst forward.

When I raced across the castle this time, Clara wasn't clinging to my back in wondrous laughter. Fearful intuition fueled every pounding footstep as I bolted up stairs, dove around wall-top guards, slid over or beneath obstructions, and maintained the fastest speed I'd ever run in my life.

Craven Keep seemed to rise ever higher as I rushed towards it, as if it were defiantly mocking me. *No point in waiting on the elevator,* I realized. *Fastest way is to go back the way I came before...*

The fact that I couldn't read the hearts of any of the passing guards added insult to injury. *I have to take better care of her,* I told myself. *Once I know that she's safe, I'll do* everything *within my power to keep that the case...*

My thumping footfalls finally brought me to the base of the tower's ascension. I dove onto the nearby battlement and sprung up onto the round wall of Craven Keep. Keeping my momentum, I rushed up the outside edge of the stone. There was no ignoring the strain on my muscles as I desperately raced higher and higher, rushing up around the tower in the same spiral as I had when she was riding on my back.

With one powerful burst, I lunged up towards the closest sill of my bedroom. Fortunately, the window was open, so I didn't even have to break the glass to get in.

"Clara?" I called for her, shoving through the drapes and bolting into my private suite. "Clara, where are–"

I froze in place. Broken glass and ripped pages were scattered across the den. They showed the signs of a clear and evident struggle, leading from the dining table to the staircase door, swinging on its hinge. From where I stood, the swaying door revealed the unconscious and strewn bodies of Wilhelm, Viktor, and Assara.

Hopelessly, I sank to my knees in the debris. "Clara..." I groaned in agony. "How could this...? Who could have...?"

The slightest glint caught my attention.

I grabbed a piece of glass and lifted it before my eyes. There, on several of the broken shards, a few droplets of blood...

Wait... this can't be human blood.

Holding the jagged shard close to my nostrils, I inhaled deeply... and pulled back, looking at the jagged glass in my hand in veiled horror. Needing complete certainty, I brought the chunk of glass back to my face and inhaled even deeper.

My darkest suspicions were confirmed.

I recognize this scent...

Dropping the shard to the floor, I rose angrily to my

feet. Clara had been taken, but the struggle revealed to me who it was. Better still, the node network was mostly inactive — there was only *one* suitable place to quietly hold her hostage...

22

CLARA

The dungeon cellar stank of rot and mildew as I tried to work my wrists out of the bindings.

My captor glanced over at me. Rubbing salt in the wound, her face was the picture of sympathy. "No need to bother with all that, little human..."

Dropping to a squat in front and playfully tapping my gag with a finger, Nikki Craven gave me a mad smile with wide, innocent eyes. "You'll only chafe yourself trying to escape them. Really, it's for the best that you don't try to fight this."

I couldn't stand the guiltless look on her face. It was my blind naiveté that kept me from seeing the truth all along. Elliott hadn't trusted her since she'd arrived; he'd tried to warn me that his sister was a deranged, unstable lunatic and a threat.

If only I'd listened, I thought sadly.

Apparently satisfied, Nikki hopped back up and strolled across the room. As she peered into the hallway, I noticed that she kept nervously scratching at the inside of her wrist.

She's been doing that since we got here, I quietly observed. The pale skin of her wrist was almost bloody now from her restless scratching. For the first twenty minutes, I had been hopeful that she was just afraid of being caught. But I'd noticed her increasingly erratic behavior, and realized that I'd been wrong about *that,* too.

Nikki wasn't afraid of being found.

She *wanted* to be found.

The vampire's anxiety came from impatience. As she constantly paced the dungeon, I watched her nervous tics and twitches.

"Shouldn't be taking this long," she grunted. "*Why* is it taking this long?"

I shuddered to think what she could possibly be waiting for. Nikki turned to me, pausing in the middle of her unhinged, back-and-forth striding. "Clara, you're smart. Why is this taking so long?"

With my voice muffled, I settled for glaring at her and deadpanning the best '...Seriously?' look that I could manage.

"Oh," she chuckled cheerfully. "Right... the, uh..." Nikki chirpily pointed at her own mouth. "The gag, duh! I mean, how could I possibly forget about the gag?"

If I get out of this mess, I furiously thought, *I'm going to freaking **strangle** her.*

There was no telling how long I was trapped there with her, bored out of my mind. But when I finally heard echoing footsteps, coming from somewhere down the hall, it occurred to me that perhaps the crippling, mind-numbing boredom was the better option...

"Lady Craven, you've done well."

Wait... don't I recognize that voice...?

Nikki turned to me with a faint smile. "Little human here put up a bit of a fight, but I'm pretty sure she's figured out her place now."

Our mystery guest was still standing just out of sight from me. "Good, good... tell me, have you secured us a way out of the castle like I asked?"

"The chrysm nodes are keyed to the genetics of the royal family, and it just so happens..." Nikki came over to me and endearingly stroked her fingers through my hair. I shuddered at her vile touch. "...I'm the adoring little sister of the ruling vampire lord. I can take us away from the castle."

When the figure finally stepped into view, my eyes widened in shock.

The sorceress? What's Sabine doing here?

The traitor knelt down right in front of me. She studied my alarmed gaze with a disinterested, menacing glance. "Lady Craven, your plan is to merely teleport us out of Stonehold Castle with a restrained fugitive?" She frowned, turning over to Nikki. "We'll never make it to the chrysm nodes before they capture us."

Nikki shrugged, barely concealing a sly smile. "But don't you have all kinds of wacky magical powers? Surely, you can do some sort of trick to make her invisible or something..."

Irritation flickered across the sorceress's face as she checked the tightness of my bindings. "You have a tenuous grasp of how magic works. I don't blame you; throughout the Eight Holds, most of the ruling families suffer that lapse in judgment."

Nikki grinned. "Nope, I never went to any of those fancy schools. Turns out, holds usually take a lot of attention. Not really a lot of downtime for hobbies, you know? But speaking of the other families..." The deranged vampire's eye twitched. "Bring me up to speed here, Sabine. Are we taking her back to your master, or what?"

Terror filled me. *If Sabine has a master outside the castle...* All I could do was hope that she didn't serve one of the other vampire lords.

"My master? Well, that *was* the plan..."

"Huh?" Nikki seemed confused. "That kind of sounds very, I don't know, *past tense?*"

"Well..."

Sabine wickedly smiled, stroking the backs of her

knuckles along my cheek. I tried to pull away from her; the traitor wasn't having any of that.

"Lord Azuzi is willing to pay a pretty coin for the human girl, but I daresay things changed when I discovered her magical resistance – then she told me that she's a witch..."

My spirits completely collapsed.

Akachi Azuzi, the vampire lord of the Falvian Badlands? If that's who she called 'master', I knew that I was as good as dead.

Nikki looked bored. "Oh?"

"There isn't a creature alive that's capable of resisting magic, Lady Craven. No... this human is worth *substantially* more to me than mere coin. A few associates in Selvara Karn will help me study her... then, after I remove her spell resilience and find a way to replicate it, we'll have the biggest breakthrough since beginning the golden age of chrysm engineering."

"Selvara Karn, eh? That's across the world."

I recognized the name from my time studying the maps. *They want to take me to South America?*

Sabine finally turned away.

"It would benefit us to put as much distance as we can between us and Stonehold. No doubt, your brother will hunt us for the rest of his life."

"Actually, I plan to stay and cover your tracks. So long as you honor our deal, of course..."

"That's wise," Sabine noted. "It makes for a cleaner getaway, and you can keep your current life with none the wiser. But Elliott's chase will be all for naught. Selvarra Karn is filled with some of the oldest magic in the world. The hold is bathed in mystique for a reason. Once I take this girl across the ocean and disappear into those ancient, tribal rainforests, he will never find us..."

Nikki nodded pensively. "Will Clara survive?"

"In all likelihood?" Sabine thoughtfully folded her arms. "No, probably not. But I just need her kept *mostly* alive for a few years..."

The sorceress turned back, staring at me like a master butcher, studying a cut of prized meat.

"My friends in the lands abroad are powerful black magicians, gifted in extraction. With their help, I should be able to keep her in at least a state of *unlife* until I can rip her magical resistance out. After that, I might very well sell whatever's left of the human on the Forbidden Markets."

Elliott's sister glanced over at me again with that same, pitying glance of sympathy. *Especially after their casual chat, I want nothing more than to slap that stupid look right off her face...*

But I'll never get the chance, will I?

"Well, consider me satisfied," Nikki tilted her head in a maniac grin. "Think I've heard enough. Let's make the magic happen."

The traitorous sorceress heartily chuckled. "Lady Craven, such a way with words you have. From the moment you first approached me, I had a feeling you could be an interesting partner... let's make the magic happen, indeed."

My eyes were glued to Elliott's sister. I sensed something suddenly very different about her, and it captivated my attention.

Nikki sadistically grinned.

"Oh, I was being very literal, Sabine..."

With a quick, rolling motion of her wrists, she clicked both sets of fingers right after the other. In an instant, bright symbols flared up around the room, all over the walls and floor.

The sorceress glanced around in total panic.

"Binding sigils? But... how?"

When she noticed her partner's triumphant grin, she was blatantly furious. "Nikki? How can you possibly... *what have you done?*"

My eyes weren't on Sabine anymore.

Nikki Craven struck fear in my heart; within just a few seconds, her entire demeanor darkened in complete fury, only made more sinister by her tenuous grip on sanity.

"I've spent countless decades wandering this hold in a beggar's disguise. Do you honestly think I don't know how to spot a sleeper agent?"

Her voice dropped to a menacing growl at Sabine's stunned expression. "Don't act surprised. Did you honestly think that you're the only one? I've discovered, tracked, and punished traitors from nearly every hold. But of course, only *Akachi Azuzi* would be daring enough to try and put a converted traitor on the Isle of Obsidian...

"I love my brother, but Elliott was a damned fool to give out an open invitation to the castle. His fear for Clara's safety blinded his judgment. Believe me, I saw somebody like *you* coming from kilometers away. All I had to do was get here first and bide my time until you showed up..."

Sabine furiously growled, throwing up her hands to cast a spell. To her great horror, nothing happened; she snarled in blind rage.

"We could have made a fantastic team, you and I! The incredible things we could have done! But you just *had* to throw it all away, you stupid, deranged, *miserable* little—"

The maddened vampire dove for her before she could finish. The two of them crumpled down to the ground in a barrage of flinging fists and biting fangs. I could barely tell who had the upper hand – but the sister of the vampire lord had kept the element of surprise on her side all along, and she'd quickly overwhelming the *real* threat.

It stunned me how well she'd played her role.

While the two were distracted, I tried to work my wrists out of my bindings again. Of course, it was an exercise in futility – but I still had to *try*.

Sabine managed to get the advantage. With a swift kick, she sent Nikki across the floor. It was just enough time for the sorceress to scramble to her feet, erasing a few chalk sigils with her sleeve.

Nikki flung herself to her feet and rushed my betrayer again, tackling Sabine into the wall with a furious roar. The sorceress slid down the surface and launched herself back, pinning Nikki against another wall as they battled.

To my horror, I realized that their grappling against the walls was brushing away more of the chalk. The evil glint in Sabine's eyes told me that she noticed this. Clearly, Nikki did not. She only continued to take every opportunity to punish the sorceress against the stones. Blinded with fury, she didn't notice how their physical fighting was slowly wiping away all the sigils...

I tried to warn her, but all that I could manage were mumbled shrieks. If they kept this up, half of them would be gone soon – and there was no telling how many it took to bind Sabine's power...

They threw down near me again. This time, the fighting brushed against me, and I felt myself slowly slide down the wall and wipe away yet another of the binding sigils. As I panicked into the gag in my mouth, my bound body slammed down *hard* against the floor.

The last thing I saw, as my face pressed into the stone, was a familiar shadow in the doorway. Elliott Craven was here, startled by the sight. But to my complete horror, his murderous glare was focused entirely on his *sister*...

23

ELLIOTT

I was untethered, and my rage knew no bounds.

Flinging myself into the room, I suddenly felt incredibly weakened. My boots stumbled against the wet stone and I gasped for air. Everything was dim and hazy for a moment, but the bright lights scrawled across the entire cell stuck out to me.

Binding sigils...

Crudely drawn in chalk, the symbols glowed ominously across every wall. In my studies, I'd seen marks like these before; they were meant to dampen magical power – *all* magical power.

The effect seemed to amplify for me.

Even worse, the sigils seemed to be canceling out the extrasensory awareness I normally gained by being near Clara. I could feel them numbing my mind and blurring my thoughts...

Nobody in the room seemed to even notice me. Clara looked out for the count; the other two were too preoccupied with their grappling brawl. In the fracas, they were both reduced to punching and clawing like savage animals.

It didn't matter.

Saving Clara was the important part...

They finally noticed me as I reached my girl. She'd smacked her head against the stone and was in a slight daze, but she was breathing.

"Lord Elliott!" Sabine desperately gasped from behind me. "Help me! Your sister's trying to take Clara away and sell her to—"

She was cut off by the sound of a hard boot connecting with soft flesh. "Silence, traitor!"

Ignoring them both, I scooped Clara up off of the ground in my arms. Her limp body dangled as I took a stumbling step forward, desperate to get both of us out of the radius of the sigils.

Sabine gasped from behind. "Lord Elliott...!"

I grunted, feeling the slightest sensation of a burden lifting from my shoulders. The dungeons were a little clearer now; I could see that I hadn't even been walking us towards the door after all.

"My Lord, if you'd just turn around..."

I vowed to personally deal with my sister's betrayal once I'd gotten Clara to safety. The only priority to me was getting her out of here. Once I was a little further out of the sigils' radius, I could think clearer...

"Elliott Craven, take another step and die."

I stopped in an instant.

With a furious grunt, I gently lowered Clara to the floor; I turned around to face the vile source of that imminent threat.

Sabine stood poised over the slumped body of my sister, her glowing hands raised defensively. "You *really* should have listened to me, Elliott. If you'd helped me deal with her, it wouldn't have needed to come to this..."

My vacant, heavy stare lowered to Nikki. Her defeated form looked pitiful under Sabine's robes. Trace marks of a few spells left bruises and marks against her pale skin, and I began to slowly piece things together.

Stoically, I lifted my weary gaze to Sabine's smug smile. Nikki might have abducted Clara, but it was obvious now that she hadn't been the true danger here. Clearly, in her insanity she'd tried to devise some trap that had gone wildly wrong...

"Tell me why," I commanded her.

Sabine's confident grin only grew even wider. "Let's be crystal clear on this, *my Lord*..." her voice took a mocking tone. "I really don't have to follow *any* order you give me, *especially* not anymore."

"Humor me, then. It's apparent you didn't get this far alone; don't pretend it was with the help of the woman at your feet." I scowled at Nikki's slumped body again. "I ask that you grant me the satisfaction, sorceress, of learning who ultimately enabled you to betray me."

Sabine smiled wickedly. "Lord Azuzi."

"Ah," I nodded thoughtfully. Mulling over the revelation, I replied: "It seems so obvious now..."

"I was exiled from the Falvian Badlands many years ago," Sabine informed me. "I've stayed here in Stonehold, waiting patiently through *centuries* for the opportunity to earn my place back in Lord Azuzi's court..."

Her attention drifted to the unconscious body behind me. *This sorceress has proven herself quite the bad luck charm for Clara, hasn't she?*

"My true master promised me a handsome reward, if were I to bring him the human. But that was before I discovered her special resistance to magic, and when she told me she had a witch's lineage, well..." Sabine shrugged. "Plans change."

A witch's lineage? My gaze slid back to Clara. *I'll have to ask her about that soon...*

"And my sister?"

"Nikki attempted to trick me with an alliance. She might have even beaten me, but I made sure that our fight rubbed away enough of the sigils to reclaim some of my power. I may still be weak, but it's enough to deal with her..."

Her menacing stare lingered.

"And plenty enough to deal with *you*..."

Within a single stride, I crossed the room; in the blink of an eye, my elbow found itself lodged deep into her stomach.

"Wh-wha–?" She gasped for air.

"The sigils weakened my power too, as you've clearly noticed," I hissed in her ear. "When your strength began dripping back into your veins, my foolish sorceress... *so did mine.*"

When I yanked my elbow free from her, she cradled her abdomen in pain. With a violent snarl, Sabine gnarled the fingers of both hands, drawing them to her sides and preparing to try and strike me down in a burst of magic.

"Fool!" Sabine laughed maniacally. "The meek strength of the world's youngest vampire lord is *nothing* to a sorceress of war! To a sorceress of the Court of the Falvian Badlands!"

But she didn't get the chance to attack.

Nikki spun a kick out from beneath, dropping Sabine to the floor around her. My sister lunged up, delivering a powerful kick to her skull.

"You idiot! I am cloaked in shielded magic!" Sabine snapped as she rebelliously hopped back to her feet. But she didn't get a change to counter; I grabbed her by her wrist and hurled her across the dungeon cell.

The sorceress slammed against the opposite wall and crumpled against the unforgiving floor. It would only be a small matter of time before her failing magical shield was completely gone.

"I... will kill... you *both*..."

Nikki defiantly rose beside me.

We shared a silent glare before turning on the weakened sorceress. Unsteadily, Sabine crackled an arc of lightning in the air towards us; Nikki slid below as I flipped above it. Both of us effortlessly dodged the blast, and the next, and the third, until we descended together upon our enemy.

"*No!*" Sabine roared in her wrath; she readied her burning palms to scorch both of us alive in a powerful blast. "All the time that I've waited for this! *I won't let you take this away from me!*"

Nikki threw up her wrist in an arc, clicking her fingers to deflect the fireball. I dove in the gap after it, throwing my arms around the sorceress to restrain her the old-fashioned way as I dropped to a kneeling position at her back. My sister was right behind me, drawing a pair of fingers in the air in a specific motion as she splayed her free hand across Sabine's head.

She screamed: "*You can't do this to me!*"

The sorceress fought my embrace, but I had too strong a grip. Filled with an eternal hatred, she glared daggers up at my sister; Nikki chanted a quick incantation as she matched the traitor's righteous anger with the same uncompromising level of passion.

"It doesn't matter!" Sabine descended into evil laughter. "You can't stop my master! Even as I fail, even as my chance at greatness is ripped from my grasp, Azuzi Akachi will destroy you all—"

With her fingers still splayed around Sabine's head, Nikki uttered the final syllable. The instant she finished chanting, the sorceress's eyes flew open as her skull recoiled from magical whiplash. Her body went completely limp in my arms.

I released my tight grip on Sabine, letting her flop limply against the floor. Dusting myself off, I rose to my feet. "Tell me you didn't kill her, Nikki. I can't question a dead traitor."

"Do you think me an idiot?" My sister smirked like a maniac. "How am I supposed to take out all my anger on my enemy if she's dead? All I did was put her to sleep, just like she did to Clara. Only, my way is a little... rougher, maybe."

I glanced down at the defeated sorceress, left crumpled at my feet. "She doesn't *look* asleep..."

Nikki sighed. "Then check if she's breathing."

Following the suggestion, I held my fingers under her nose. Sure enough, Sabine's exhalations rolled over my digits in a telltale rhythm. "Fine. But that's one of the deepest sleeps I've ever seen."

"Like I said, 'just like she did to Clara.'"

I focused an irritated glance Nikki's way.

"There's no telling if she did that on purpose. Either way, I thought it fitting to magically force her into the same sort of coma," my sister noted calmly. "She will remain like this for a good few days.... long enough for you to decide what to do with her, and how to interrogate her."

"You are aware, of course, that Sabine won't be the *only* one who will be questioned," I darkly narrowed my eyes. "Those sigils took a great deal of time to draw, Nikki. You were waiting for her to arrive, and you've got a *lot* of explaining to do."

"Oh, that can wait," my sister smiled with just a hint of deviancy. "I believe your sleeping little pet over there is waking up..."

I glanced expectantly over my shoulder.

As it turned out, Nikki was right. After a few desperate strides, I was kneeling at Clara's side and ripping out her gag. Once I carefully worked her out of her bindings, I held her trembling hand in both of mine.

Clara stirred. She touched her head painfully and winced at the raw sensation. "Ah!" She hissed. "Why do I feel like I got hit with a bat...?"

"You took a small tumble," I replied. "Struck your head against the floor. It knocked you out. We'll probably have to have you checked for a concussion later..."

"If we could just *stop putting me in comas,* that would be just great." Clara saw the concerned look on my face and beamed. "You know, Elliott, you're sorta handsome when you're worried about me."

"Don't scare me like that," I replied softly.

She blinked, studying my eyes briefly. "You really *were* afraid I was in danger, weren't you?"

"Of course I was, Clara. When I came back and you had been taken, the only thing that mattered was finding and protecting you..."

"That has to be the sweetest thing anyone has ever said to me," she whispered.

"You have become irreplaceable in my life," I told her, stroking a few stray strands of hair from her face. "I'm sorry that it's taken me this long to come to terms with that, but it's true, Clara. I need you. The very thought of something happening to endanger you makes me feel a crushing fear that I've never known..."

Clara's eyes sparkled with raw emotion. The impulse to kiss her overwhelmed me, and just as I started to lean in...

"Lord Elliott!"

I was pulled from my affectionate daze as the three worst protectors in the world burst onto the scene. Wilhelm, Viktor, and Asarra froze as they saw us. Then, their shocked gaze took in the rest of the chamber's sights: the dimming sigils, my weary sister, even the crumpled sorceress...

"What *happened* here?" Viktor blurted out.

"How did you find us?" I asked suspiciously.

Wilhelm accusingly squinted at my sister. "Well, Lord Elliott, funny story there... once your *darling little psychopath* over there turned on us with some of that wacky magical business, she decided to make things okay again by jamming a couple of detailed notes in our pockets."

Viktor shook his head in disbelief. "Didn't even know she could *do* magic." He crossed his arms and expectantly turned to Wilhelm.

"What, you think *I* knew?" The knight threw his hands up in disgust. "It's madness! They don't bother to tell us *anything* anymore!"

Asarra grunted and ignored her companions. "Lady Craven's notes brought us here and pointed Sabine as a traitor. She also went out of her way to make nonsensical accusations about our mothers, and she left 'apologies' in the form of scribbling out little animal drawings."

"Mine's a duck," Wilhelm helpfully added.

"You will have to explain to me what caused you to let your guard down," I told them firmly. "But, as for now..." I turned back to Clara. "I'm just happy to see that you're alive and well."

"I always am when you're close, Elliott."

A warm smile crossed my face.

It was almost enough to silence the nagging, rising paranoia in my heart. Some part deep down knew that this couldn't last – but I needed to have this moment with her, safe and sound. Filled with relief, I pulled Clara to my chest and memorized the way her body felt pressed against mine, and how her hair smelled against my face.

She was protected for now.

And that's all I cared about.

24

ELLIOTT

The sensation of victory didn't last for long.

I was eager to put this all as far behind me as I could, and Clara clearly agreed. But it wasn't meant to be. Not even halfway through dinner, a frantic servant rushed into the dining hall.

"My Lord? Something has happened!"

I glanced over from the table, recognizing the guard as one I'd stationed in the dungeon tonight.

"It's been a very long and draining night," I carefully warned him as I begrudgingly set down my silverware. "What's the matter *now?*"

The guard was hesitant. "It's the sorceress..."

I was out of my chair in an instant and at his side. "Don't tell me she's escaped!"

"My Lord," he trembled at my mounting fury, "you

should come with me. I think you're going to want to see this for yourself..."

There was no way that I was allowing Clara out of my sight so quickly, so she accompanied me with her appointed protectors.

The chrysm node system was back online; we took the express trip down into the dungeon. My refined senses picked up the scent before we even came into view. Once we had turned the last corner and stepped into sight of Sabine's cell, I realized to my horror what had transpired here.

"Wait!" I tried to stop her. "Clara, don't—"

She threw a hand over her mouth.

"Oh my god!"

I stood between her and the cell, but I already knew the image had burned into her mind. I could only hope that time would be merciful to her; one day, I hoped, it would make Clara forget.

"Elliott, I..." She wept into my embrace.

Defensively, I held her close. "I know."

Wilhelm, Viktor, and Asarra slowly crept up to Sabine's cell in various levels of disgust. Several guards were already standing near it; our escort looked at me in sympathy before joining them.

"I have to go over there," I whispered to her.

Clara nodded tearfully. "Okay."

"Don't turn back around. I'll have the others take you wherever in the castle you'd like to go. But you should leave this place. I don't want this affecting you more than it already has. Okay?"

Staring into my eyes, she nodded.

"Good." I turned my head, still holding myself in her way. "You three. I'll take over from there."

It was a mistake to bring her down here...

Her guardians were quick to follow my order, clearly shaken by the sight. I gave a resolved nod; the three guardians quickly swarmed Clara and safely removed her from the dungeon.

As repeat waves of the overwhelming stench struck me, I vigilantly walked towards the cell.

The remaining guards parted at my approach. Scattering to the sides, they covered their faces or kept their eyes away from the gruesome sight.

I walked up to the sorceress and crouched.

At this point, Sabine's scorched remains were barely recognizable. It appeared that the magical fire burned its way out from the inside; even upon death, her blackened face had been contorted into a smug, wicked and hellish smile.

"How did this happen?" The escorting guard shook his head in total disbelief. "I mean, I don't really know my magic, but weren't all these runes here meant to *stop* her from casting spells?"

"This isn't a traditional spell," I disagreed. "All I can gather is that she had some sort of failsafe in her body. It takes something powerful to trigger a reaction like this. Apparently, our friend here was fully prepared for the possibility of capture, or the discovery of her plot..."

He shook his head. "I honestly don't like to meet *any* vampire who can smile like that while burning alive. Although, now that I *say* that..."

"Don't worry. She didn't feel pain."

"*What?* Are you kidding?"

"The magic Sabine used for this was strong enough to evade all these binding runes. It stands to reason that the traitor could craft together a triggered reaction that would spare her the pain of a gruesome death." I gloomily focused on him. "Death by immolation is a horrific way to go. You see that smile on her face? The sorceress wanted us to *know* that she didn't suffer..."

The guard looked at her again and shuddered. "You don't say... you really think so?"

"Yes," I nodded. "It's incredibly likely that one of two things happened: either Sabine's magic canceled out her pain receptors, or she enjoyed a far more peaceful passing first – before the spell burst the body left behind into flames."

I rose to my feet; I looked around at the runes.

They'd done their job, but they weren't designed for this kind of technicality. *The loophole here is that Sabine didn't have to actually **cast** anything...*

"What do you want us to do with her?"

My gaze took in the charred sight again. "She clearly wanted to taunt her captors, whoever we wound up being; her magic did an *intentionally* poor job at destroying her body."

Lost in my irritation, I frowned at the guard. "Torch the cell. There is nothing more I can learn from her defiled bones now. I want the contents of this room completely obliterated."

"Do you want her remains moved first?"

"No." I glared down at what was left of Sabine with burning hatred. "There should be no record she was ever in here. I want every last trace of her wiped from existence; and if there's *any* chance that her spirit might stay trapped where she died, then I want her ghost to rot in this disgusting dungeon cell for all eternity..."

THE GROUP OF DUNGEON GUARDS PREPARED THE CELL for total eradication, and then backed away.

At my request, they'd been thorough in their fuel stacking. Estimates put the coming blaze hot enough to scorch away any evidence of her bones. All that would stay behind was ash and crumbles.

The guards nodded among themselves.

One struck a match; another nearby turned to me with a concerned look. "My Lord, are you sure you really want to see this?"

I crossed my arms. "Do it."

The lit match sailed towards the far wall, and the entire cell burst into flames. Several guards took another step back from the inferno's sudden heat; they held up gauntleted hands, attempting to shield their faces from the blaze.

Well played, Sabine, I begrudgingly admitted. *Now, you can **never** be used against Akachi Azuzi...*

The fire roared. The blaze must have burned for half an hour, but I didn't move a muscle. I was determined to see this through to the very end.

So that's exactly what I did.

Only as the last flickering flame finally faded did I relax at last. When I re-entered the cell, the traitor's body was cleansed away in fiery baptism. All evidence of that victorious smile was gone; her very bones had been wiped from sight. There was nothing left of my betrayer but charred ashes.

"It's finally over," a guard sighed.

No, I bitterly disagreed.

I feel it's only just beginning...

25

ELLIOTT

Clara was exactly where I knew she'd be – curled up in my bed, quietly weeping in the dark.

I sat beside her and placed a hand on her back. Grief overwhelmed me as I stroked her shoulders, feeling how they rolled with her gentle sobs. In her silent sorrow, Clara was more beautiful than ever before.

The realization hit me like a brick:

I can never keep her safe here.

The other vampire lords knew she existed. It was only a matter of time before she was made an international fugitive. Acting on orders, a threat had infiltrated the castle. Worse still, I personally invited said danger into my own stronghold. This young, delicate life had been put in peril, and the only person I had to blame was myself. It seemed that nothing I'd done since her arrival had done anything but paint a bigger target on her back.

If I can't foresee a threat like this from within my own kingdom... I steeled myself. *I'll have no chance at protecting her from the other rulers of the Eight Holds. The others have made themselves clear. They'll stop at* nothing *to get their hands on her...*

Nikki was right.

War loomed on the horizon, and there would be no stopping it now. Even with the few allies I had among the vampire lords, the only testimony I had left to provide of Azuzi's treachery was that of my deranged sister – and the very human being they strove to take for themselves.

They would never listen to me. I'd lost my one and only chance at proving his culpability. When the chips finally fell, I'd stand alone. Lord Azuzi had never dared to strike against Lorelei while she sat on the throne, and he obviously considered me weak and vulnerable.

If that's the game you want to play, Akachi... My eyes narrowed in grounded conviction. *If you so desperately want to see what I'm truly capable of, I'll be more than happy to show you.*

Clara broke me from my thoughts.

She reached for my hand, taking it into hers. She pulled it to her face, and I had to lower myself down to the bed around her. "I'm so sorry, Elliott," she whispered in the dark. "If I hadn't come here, you wouldn't have to do any of this. Lorelei and you were right all along – all of you are in danger because of me."

"No," I murmured in her ear. "No, don't blame yourself for this at all. You did not sneak into my kingdom and try to steal from me. Whatever happens next, it happens because of terrible, vile people trying to abuse their power. They'll all get what is coming to them, Clara. Maybe this was inevitable; if not through you, maybe they would have struck at me another way. But it ultimately doesn't matter, because today we won."

"Did we, though?" Clara rolled over to face me in the dark. "This just feels like the beginning. If they're so willing to attack you now, what's going to stop the vampire lords from doing something even worse next time?"

"Me," I replied darkly.

"You? What do you mean, Elliott?"

"I will make Akachi Azuzi pay. He's old and feeble, and he must be taught to never challenge me again. I must send a message to the others, plain and clear, showing them all what happens when they dare to antagonize me."

Clara shook her head. "I don't like the sound of that. This vengeance, this anger... that's not the Elliott Craven I've grown to know and adore."

*Then perhaps **that** Elliott Craven is overdue to finally grow up,* I reasoned silently.

"Lord Azuzi has broken the peace. Whether or not they believe me, I must make it clear that I'll tolerate *nothing* like what happened today. If I don't, they'll come to see me as a weak ruler, and they'll take advantage. That goes double if I have something they want – something like a human."

Clara emotionally sank down into herself. "I know... but there's got to be a better way, Elliott."

"If there is, I'll find it."

"*We'll* find it," she whispered quietly, pulling my wrist to her face. Clara planted a small kiss on the knuckles. "Together."

The knife twisted in my heart as I lied to her.

"...Together."

※

TOSSING AND TURNING IN GRIEF, I COULD BARELY REST that night. The fact that Clara managed to sleep through it at all was a small wonder unto itself.

The dawn came, but I was already awake. For once, I watched how the rising light drifted into the room, bathing it in the dim glow of early sun. Since I'd had all night to think, the drapes had been pulled aside for that very purpose.

Satisfied, I rose from the bed and pulled them back shut. Clara barely murmured as I sat on the edge of the bed and admired her sleeping form.

She was so beautiful. The thought of losing her to that horrible fate – disappearing across the world into some dark and distant hold – tugged at my heartstrings.

My trembling fingers stroked her hair lightly, indulging in the feeling of her tenderness. *I can't ever let that happen to her.* Above all else, even with the distance of that bed, I wanted nothing more than to rest with her. The warmth of Clara's body near mine was utterly intoxicating, and not just because of her blood.

There was no denying it any longer.

I loved her.

In my heartache, I sighed with responsibility. After all, I was still the vampire lord of Stonehold. Regardless of my personal life and its tragedies, I had a duty to uphold to my people.

Pausing to give her a quick peck on her cheek, I turned and left her to finish her slumber. The last thing I recalled from the night before, just as we drifted to sleep, was that Clara asked me to let her talk to my sister. I'd been so beside myself with regret that I'd allowed it, but now that morning had come, I reconsidered the wisdom behind that choice.

Well, it was important to her, I remembered. *Nikki has made her true alliances clear, I suppose...*

As the day slowly dragged on, I forced myself to go through the motions.

For over an hour, listened to Silas' rambling. Afterwards, I oversaw the inspection of several barracks and stockpiles around the castle. Later in the day, I even sat down with several advisors to work out some sort of fairer taxation system.

But in all these things, I was barely there.

I skipped lunch. I avoided my family.

In my dark and troubled state, I found myself wandering the castle towards the late afternoon. By now, most of my staff was aware of what had happened; I was given either a wide berth, or faint and sympathetic smiles.

To be honest, I was eager to be rid of them all. It felt impossible to clear my head with almost constant company. So, I sought out a remote and quiet place for some peace and quiet.

I teleported down into the sage's library, and my feet aimlessly took me forward. I had no true idea what I expected to find down here now, so I wandered towards Sebastian's office. Even in my anti-social state, I considered him a guiding voice that I could never refuse. *Perhaps he can offer me some wisdom on the matters that plague me...*

His office stood empty and abandoned.

Disappointed, I quietly wandered throughout the countless bookcases. Shelves upon shelves of endless tomes greeted me; I just couldn't pull the energy to pluck one from its place, finding a place of respite to read it.

After a short while, I came across a small area designed for seated study. I slumped down into an ancient, dusty armchair, finally letting myself sink and wallow in my pained thoughts...

Hours passed; I know not how many.

"My Lord?"

I stirred, unaware of how long I'd been there. To my small surprise, Sage Sebastian stood before me with a thick book under his arm. I recognized it as the same one he'd used before; within those pages, he'd found the magic that almost cured us all of our bloodlust for Clara...

"Sebastian?" I asked drowsily.

"Lord Elliott..." the sage hesitated reluctantly. "I believe I may have found the answer to all your problems. But I must warn you, what I am about to tell you involves a great deal of sacrifice..."

I sat up wearily in my seat, waving away his fears. "You have already done so much; I wouldn't dream of asking you to forgo anything else."

"Were it so easy..." he solemnly replied. As his words trailed off, the sage looked at me much like I'd expect a father might; his eyes were filled with a great and loving reluctance.

"The sacrifice must be *yours,* Lord Elliott."

26

CLARA

Sleeping fitfully with horrible dreams of danger, I didn't wake up until very late in the afternoon.

Of course, Elliott was gone.

Expecting him to spend the entire day in bed with me wasn't exactly reasonable. I still hoped I could wake up beside him, one of these days. But he stayed so distracted with his responsibilities as a powerful ruler. It didn't help that it sounded more and more like his education for it was built on the concept of 'trial by fire.'

As I lay in bed, I wondered instead when I might see Lorelei again. I wanted to talk to her more about her fears for the future, and why she abdicated the throne. *Maybe she'll think I've grown up a little more, especially after what just happened.* I questioned if she'd be more forthcoming now, as if she'd think the experience toughened me up.

I heard her voice: *The black wind howls...*

I'd been able to think these things without having to deal with the aftermath, but it couldn't last. Terrible snippets of my harrowing night snapped back to memory with a vengeance. The events still took their toll on me, both physically and spiritually. *If Elliott hadn't intervened when he did, that horrible sight of the sorceress could have burned into my mind...* But, thanks to him, I'd gotten nothing more than a fleeting glance at the dungeon cell and its grisly contents.

The picture was just as short-lived to me now as my old nightmare. It seemed strange to me that entire days had passed without me thinking–

I bolted up in bed, remembering my dream.

Terror flooded my heart. I lifted a trembling hand to my face, holding back tears as I suddenly remembered the images that had spent the entire night assaulting my mind.

It was the forest nightmare again.

It had never occurred to me to really question that it vanished once I'd arrived here. Even telling Lorelei about it, in the building days before the spell, had done nothing to bring it back.

"Why?" I gasped aloud. "Why *now*?"

The fact that it was back sent a shudder down my spine, and I feared the implications. It felt like another warning. *But how,* I wondered fearfully. *It's a day late. The danger came for me last night...*

On the one hand, at least I was actually in the same *world* as the shadowy silhouette that always protected me within the nightmare; on the other, I couldn't shake the foreboding of what it meant that it had returned...

No matter how ridiculous it sounded, it felt as if the dream had *found* me. It was as if the dream had spent all this time searching for me, since I'd been off of my own Earth for so long...

You know, I thought as I blew hair out of my face, *it's funny how much just a few weeks can really change a person.*

※

AFTER I CLEANED MYSELF UP, I STEPPED INTO Elliott's suite. Wilhelm and Viktor were passed out cold on the couch; their stern companion was sitting idly at the table and staring off into space.

With the recent thrills, I'd forgotten all about that particular talent of theirs.

"Being a member of the royal guard can get awfully dull," Wilhelm had contentedly explained the day that we first met. *"Think about it: you are* always *standing at attention,* always *alert and cautious. You can imagine how, say, three hundred years of that can get a tad... droll."*

"That's right," I recalled aloud as I watched Asarra snap back to reality at my presence. They probably did this all the time while I was deep in a book, and I just didn't notice. "You were 'treated'. *All* of you were 'treated'..."

The knight cricked her neck. "That is correct. The treatments, they are sometimes convenient. Some people say boredom is the greatest curse of long life. But not for me, thanks to the treatments. Boredom shall never come for me again. When it tries, well..." Her eyes drifted to me. "I say 'no.' I turn myself off until it stops."

The idea still made me really uncomfortable. I felt ashamed that I'd even forgotten about it in the first place, and I wondered what it might take to convince my beloved vampire lord to abolish the practice outright.

He's got enough to worry about for now... that conversation can wait until later.

Asarra meaningfully looked over at the other two. Her face was always stoic, never expressive; of all the vampires I'd met here, she was the one I could never hope to read.

"What are you thinking?" I asked her.

She glanced back. "It is unimportant."

I didn't agree, but I knew better than to try to push that point. Even counting my experiences back home in England, this woman was the most insular, closed-off person I'd ever met in my life.

Instead, I made her a simple request.

"Can you find Nikki for me, Asarra?"

The knight gave me an incredulous glance. Her reply came in a flat tone. "You are not serious. You *cannot* be serious."

I couldn't help a smile. "I am, actually."

"But... Lady Craven attacked us. She removed you from our care. Do you have, what do they call it?" Her Eastern European accent grew even more endearing with her frustration. "A death wish?"

"No," I smiled. "I don't have one of those."

"Then... I do not understand."

I leaned toward her with a knowing smile, partly bent over the dining table. "Asarra, did you ever figure out why I wanted Wilhelm and Viktor to protect me, even though they put me in danger once before?" I tilted my head with interest. "Or maybe why I requested *you*, too, even though you forcibly captured me when I first arrived?"

"No," she muttered. "Why is that?"

"Because I forgave you, Asarra," I enlightened her. "I forgave *all* of you. In your own little ways, all of you do what you think is right. I know none of you intended to ever really cause me any strife. You all care about me, but you show it differently. I trust you all enough to let my life stay in your hands, and that includes Nikki." I winked with endearment. "Even if I've gotta admit that some of you are *way* better at it than others."

She stiffened in her chair, tightly pursing her lips. On anyone else's face, you could barely tell she was flustered; considering the young guard's self-control, it spoke volumes of her emotions.

"Wilhelm and Viktor acted poorly before, yes. They almost got you killed. An innocent man had to be punished because of their stupidity. You are silly in the head, Clara. You are too silly in the head for your own good." I could definitely sense her annoyance, but her delightful accent and unusual grasp of the language was honey to my ears. "Lady Craven, she did the same thing. They are all brash. They are all people who should know better, and yet they make dumb mistakes."

"Everybody makes mistakes."

"Some, eh. More than others, I think."

"You're probably right," I conceded. "But I get a good feeling about you, and them, and even her. I can't really explain it, Asarra. I wish I could. The only way I can describe it is that... well, I guess something just tells me I need all of you around. So I asked Elliott for it."

"But you still want *idiot* Wilhelm and *boring* Viktor to protect you?" Asarra laughed. "You must have, how do you say... *death wish* after all..."

My fingers absentmindedly caressed the dark necklace around my throat, dangling within my clothes. It felt heavier somehow, but only a little. "Trust me, I really don't want to die. But I can't help feeling that all of you give my best chance at staying safe... yes, even Nikki Craven." Giving her my most endearing smile, I lifted my eyebrows. "As your friend, Asarra, I'm asking you to bring her to me. I want to talk to her."

The guard went quiet. "As your friend?"

"Of course. You're all my friends! What other friends could you possibly think that I even *have* on this world?"

Pensively, she gazed off into space. "Friends. I have not... thought of it like this." Asarra slipped into a brief, contemplative state. Her eyes visibly saddened; I placed a tender hand on her shoulder. When she didn't flinch or try and brush me off, I felt the closeness warm up my heart.

"There was a moment there where I lost faith in Nikki Craven," I admitted to her. "*Of course* I thought she'd turned on me; she overpowered the three of you, took me away to a dungeon, and started acting even crazier than I've ever seen her.

"But the reality was a lot more complicated. Nikki exposed a threat in the castle; she just chose to use me to do it. I'll leave it up to everyone else to decide whether what she did was right, but I know her heart is in the right place... I can feel it.

"She deserves my forgiveness, Asarra."

The guard watched me carefully. When it was clear I wasn't changing my mind, she bowed her head in resignation. "Fine. I will do this. But we must wake the others.

Wilhelm and I will look in different places, and Viktor will watch you."

I beamed a smile and threw my arms around her. "I know you don't understand. But thank you for going along with this, Asarra."

"Wilhelm is right," she shook her head while I held her close. Especially for *her*, I sensed warmth in her even tone. "You are a very peculiar human, Clara Blackwell…"

<hr />

VIKTOR AND I DIDN'T TALK MUCH IN THE HOUR IT took them to find her.

He looked exhausted. I let him spend most of our time together staring into space while I idly flipped through my book. Somehow, the thrill of being thrust into danger had sort of tarnished my excitement for finishing the story.

When they *did* arrive with her, Nikki looked sheepish at Asarra's calm, collected side. "There," the knight grunted. "I have found Lady Craven."

Nikki glanced at me like a pitiful dog with her tail between her legs. "Hullo, Clara…"

"Hey, would you guys mind letting me talk to her in private?" I asked, taking her surprised hand in mine. "You can follow along behind like before when Lorelei asked for me, but I want privacy."

The Knightly Trio shared a look. "Sure, I mean why not?" The usually cheerful Wilhelm shook his head. "At this rate, if Lord Elliott has anything to say about it, today is gonna outlast me!"

"That is not so good an idea," Asarra replied.

"Consider it the same as Lorelei's request."

"Her Royal Highness didn't have you almost passed off to a traitor," Viktor narrowed his eyes. "*Or* hit all of us with incapacitation spells."

"Sorry about that," Nikki guiltily tried to grin. "Hopefully, the sluggish after-effects will wear off soon. Although *you* in particular look more than a little worse for wear..."

When Viktor leveled a weary, angry glare her way, Nikki evaded it by turning back to Wilhelm with a twisted smile. "I hope you at least liked my apology drawings? I worked really hard on them."

Wilhelm smirked, unable to contain himself. "Actually, the duck was a nice touch."

The insane vampire evilly returned his grin.

"Focus," Asarra harshly snapped at Wilhelm. When his smile dropped, she turned back to me. "Why is this important to you, Clara? You *know* that Lord Elliott will be angry if we say yes."

"*Angry* is an understatement," Viktor noted.

"Just trust me," I reassured her.

The faces of the Knightly Trio, even Wilhelm, cycled

through various stages of complete bother. "You know what?" The merry knight shrugged. "I don't even *care* at this point. I'm already screwed. If Lord Elliot doesn't have my head by afternoon, it'll be a total miracle!"

I gratefully hugged all three of them. "I can't thank you guys enough. Just follow us behind and keep an eye out." Teasingly, I threw an angry look at my guest. "And if *this one* tries anything, just go ahead and carve her to pieces..."

Surprising literally nobody in the room, Nikki Craven deviously grinned at the sound of that.

"*Now* we're talking."

27

CLARA

After waking up on a dungeon floor and sleeping off a horrible recurring nightmare, the last thing I wanted was to spend any more time indoors.

Nikki shrugged. "Want a walk with a view?"

"Actually... that sounds wonderful."

After a quick elevator ride down Craven Keep and fifteen minutes of walking later, that's how we wound up along the battlements. From atop the guarded walkways we could see the bustling little village within Stonehold Castle, gaze over to the surrounding woods, or glance up at the starry mid-afternoon sky.

"I still can't believe that you get stars during the day here," I gasped. "I'll never be used to that."

Nikki looked up too. "That's right! The human world

doesn't have that, does it? That sounds so boring... so then, what's *your* sky like?"

I'd never had to think of how to describe it.

"Well... it's usually a deep, rich light blue. On some days, there isn't a cloud up there, and it's like a gigantic, lifeless ocean above us. Other days, the whole thing turns into this sea of puffy white clouds. They can be stringy and strewn all over the place, or in these grand, hulking masses that are just so impossibly huge that they make you feel tiny in comparison."

Nikki smirked. "That sounds fantastic."

I finally looked down from that mesmerizing view to reply. "Don't you get any of that here?"

"You can always see the stars, Clara."

It was true that they'd been out every time I'd been able to see the sky. *I guess I'd get tired of them too, if they never actually went away...* I started to realize how my bland-by-comparison sky might sound exotic to the denizens of this world.

We pulled our attention away. Staying at her side, I began to stroll with Nikki Craven along the stone walkways atop the castle walls. I found myself avoiding the passing glances of patrolling guards and busy workers.

Every so often, I spared a brief look over my shoulder for the Knightly Trio. Strangely, I didn't spot Wilhelm – the only ones following us seemed to be Viktor and

Asarra, sticking back but looking very ready to close the distance in a heartbeat.

After a few minutes, I broke the silence.

"So, I guess you can do magic?"

Nikki smiled faintly. "Sure can."

"And it never occurred to you to perform that 'stop trying to drink Clara' spell on me *because...*"

"Well, I'm... not very good at it."

I scoffed lightheartedly. "Sure, okay. *I* think you did pretty well, going up against a powerful sorceress. Unless I'm mistaken, not a whole lot of people can do that and live to tell the tale."

"You aren't *exactly* wrong," Nikki shrugged noncommittally. "But the only way I could pull it off was with those binding runes. And from what I heard, they didn't even properly manage to do the job in the end..."

I shuddered and tried to avoid thinking about Sabine's ultimate fate.

"You see, Clara, my magic is instinctual; I put those runes there to stop her spells just as much as my own."

"Why's that?"

Nikki cut me a serious look.

"Do you really want to know?"

"I wouldn't ask if I didn't."

The vampire sighed wearily and lowered her face. Her platinum gold hair hid it from view until she looked up at me again.

"You should know that I wasn't *born* crazy."

The grave expression on her face dared me to ask, although I couldn't help but worry. "Oh?"

By now, I'd been around the deeply disturbed Nikki Craven for long enough to see that she had her moments of sharpened clarity; whenever they came, her demeanor switched, like day and night. It wasn't quite the same sort of thing as multiple personality syndrome, but there was something undeniably difficult to pin down with the special blend of crazy that she had.

"Did something happen to you, Nikki?"

Her solemn eyes deepened in powerful regret. "Yeah," the vampire whispered sadly. "I guess you could probably put it like that."

What do I say? I wanted to offer her comfort somehow, but I was at a total loss. *What can I do?*

Nikki Craven took a few short steps away; she wrapped her fingers around a railing and silently leaned against it for support. I had never seen her so utterly broken before.

As her haunted gaze drifted into the distance, I quietly took a spot next to her. Instinctively, I dared to place my hand over hers.

"You can tell me," I reassured her.

That's when I noticed that Nikki was crying. I stayed quiet, following her gaze over her mother's beautiful gardens. It made for a solemn backdrop to the sudden weight of our conversation.

"My magic," she whispered. "Like I told you a moment ago, it's instinctive. I can't control it well. When I get too angry, or scared, or if I feel danger, I lose my grip on it and it... works without me."

I nodded sympathetically.

"It happened nearly a century ago."

I sensed her fear. "What happened?"

Nikki kept her attention forward, focusing on the gardens below. Her clenched fist on the rail spasmed under my touch; she distantly released her grip and held my hand, but she was careful to not crush it in her grasp.

Even then, I noticed that Nikki wouldn't turn away from Lorelei's gardens below us. She tightly clamped her eyes shut, holding back more tears. "A century ago," she repeated gravely from the deepest throes of despair. "That's when Fiona died in the accident."

"Fiona?" I blinked. "Who's Fiona?"

She opened her eyes again, tearfully staring at the flower hedges. "Our older sister... I killed her."

<hr />

Nikki Craven's words struck me to my core.

"Elliott and you... you had an older sister?"

Her face lowered beneath the weight of a dark and

powerful depression. The fleeting traces of a demented smile twitched at her lips, but she was in too deep for them to take hold. "Yes, Clara. My brother wasn't the oldest of our generation. Fiona came one hundred thirty years earlier."

I struggled to process this. *Elliott said that she went on a self-imposed exile about a century ago... if some awful tragedy happened, then Nikki must have just run away...*

"Is it okay if I ask what happened?"

She blinked away a tear. "Yeah. I'll tell you."

After she briefly leaned against the railing and composed herself, Nikki let out a deep sigh. "It was an argument. The worst part is that I can't even remember what started the stupid thing."

She paused briefly, holding her gaze over the gardens. The starry night sky was just beginning to twinkle over us; as it settled over the area, its supernatural glow made the majestic courtyards look even better than before.

"Guess it doesn't really matter anymore," she shrugged. "We were in the middle of a fight. It got out of hand. Hurtful things were shouted – things that I guess neither of us can take back now.

"Fiona was always like that. She never backed down, never accepted defeat. Everything had to be her way. I suppose I wasn't really much better at the time."

I nodded empathetically. "Fiona Craven, huh? Guess that makes you Fiona, Elliott, and Nikki..."

"That's right. No idea how Mother dealt."

"So what was Fiona like?"

Nikki grinned to herself. "Defiant. Rebellious. Always headstrong... she took on all challengers. Our sister was a true warrior at heart. She always bit off more than she could chew. But when you thought she was down for the count, she'd figure out some ridiculous way to still come out ahead."

"It sounds like you really admired her, Nikki."

The vampire's grin faintly buckled. "We both did. Elliott and I... well, we always looked up to her. Fiona helped take care of us while we were young. For all her eagerness for battle, she didn't have a diplomatic bone in her body. Instead, she taught us to fight; she taught us to never back down from a threat, to take what was rightfully ours."

"She sounds awesome," I smiled sadly.

Nikki snorted. "Mother always thought Fiona was lucky. She even started coming to our sister's sparring matches, once Fiona began channeling her lust for challenge into physical combat. After she started routinely humbling the royal guards, it became a rite of passage to face her in the field. The whole reason we invested in a medical bay is because she showed no mercy to her enemies..."

"I'm gonna be honest, she sounds hardcore."

She laughed heartily. "That's one word for it." Nikki's

mirth slowly faded from her expression. "Everyone in the entire hold knew that, someday, Fiona Craven would sit on the Stonehold throne. But overpowering your problems is only one way of solving them. Lorelei wanted to tame the rage in her daughter's heart and teach her diplomacy."

Nikki started doing a great impersonation of her mother. 'Fiona Craven, you'll sit on the throne for over five centuries! Not every threat can be so easily *punched into submission!*'

It was my turn to laugh. I could easily picture Lorelei wagging an angry finger with her furious and almost indifferent expression.

"So, if it was an argument you two had..."

The vampire sighed again. "I couldn't control my magic. It spiraled out of my grasp. All I really remember is how much I struggled to hold myself together."

Nikki released her free hand from along the rail, flexing it open and closed. "I felt it building, Clara. I felt it rising inside me... so full of hate and anger. I tried to put some distance between the two of us, but Fiona didn't care for *the coward's retreat*, as she called it. It wasn't enough for her to not back down. She needed *us* to not back down, either. Our sister was headstrong to a fault, and she never really listened to us...

"Then... one minute she was there, shouting in my

face and holding back from hitting me..." Her face grew pained. "And then the next..."

The implication hung over the hard silence that followed. The heaviness of our conversation choked in my lungs and at the base of my throat, but I wasn't willing to stand down from this.

Nikki Craven was baring her soul to me, in the most coherent state I'd ever seen her; through the spasms of her trembling hand, I could clearly feel just how hard she had to mentally cling to her current level of clarity.

"Then she was gone," I finished for her.

Nikki's lip feebly twitched as the tears started to flow. "Elliott doesn't talk about it," she bitterly added. "Same goes for Lorelei. Neither of them let me bring up the accident. After our mother found me sobbing and cradling my sister's body, I think it snapped something inside her."

"What do you mean?"

Nikki finally looked at me. "Why do you think she became obsessed with planting this garden?"

It hit me like a stack of bricks.

"Fiona loved flowers," she noted sadly.

"So the gardens are for Fiona?"

"They were originally going to be a present for her, a way of showing her what can be made without always trying to conquer your problems with violence. But now?" Nikki glanced over them again. "Now, they're more of a memorial..."

Everything was starting to make sense now. I turned away, overcome with emotion.

"They might tell this part of the story better," Nikki continued. "My family, I mean. The magic *did* something to me that day..."

"Something like what?"

She gazed up at the starry sky.

Darkness was slowly falling across the castle. The sky gradually darkened with it, bringing that now-familiar mixture of dark purples and bright, sparkling pinks and reds. The night sky twinkled with an abundance of beautiful stars, bathing the tragic Nikki Craven under its shadow.

"I can't always fight it," she muttered. "I don't *want* to be a danger to the people around me... but when tragedy mixes with magic, it has a habit of fundamentally changing you." Nikki lowered her face and stared ominously at me. "It becomes a complex problem when you're born with innate magic that's infected with madness. There's just no stopping it now. I can't turn it off. Clara. My natural power courses through my veins, but for the past century it's been fueled by sorrow and total chaos..."

In the descending darkness, her radiant eyes shone

with a devious glint. She took a long stride towards me; I stood my ground and held her gaze.

"My darling little snack," Nikki sadly smirked, lifting my chin with a finger. She studied my eyes with a dulled smile. "You don't have an ounce of fear in there, do you now? Even with me..."

"Of course I'm scared, Nikki. At least a little," I quietly admitted to her. "But I believe that fear and courage can share the same space. I think that you're afraid too. I think you're afraid of what you think you'll become."

"Your courage may get you in trouble..."

"Maybe. I'm young. I'm pretty reckless. Maybe Asarra is right, and I forgive too easily. But I don't let the fear get in the way of my courage. Which is why I can look you in the eyes and tell you the one thing you've never heard. The thing I think that you've needed most."

She tilted her head, licking a fang. Clearly, her coherency was slipping – judging by the look in her eye, Nikki was growing madder by the second. "And what might *that* be, little human?"

"That I won't give up on you."

The devilish mirth slipped off Nikki Craven's face as she heard the words. She stared down into my eyes, and for the first time her gaze was a pane of two-way glass.

In her desolate eyes I saw the crushing fear, the bitter

abandonment, the fierce betrayal, and all of her painful longing. I gazed deep down into her salted wounds and the thorns so mindlessly driven into her torn, broken spirit.

With that moment I felt as if, for once, I truly understood this tragic creature who had slyly threatened on so many times to drink my blood or treat me like a mere pet.

Nikki Craven suddenly pulled me into her embrace, holding me tight against her chest with a hand clutching the back of my skull.

"I will never hurt you, Clara Blackwell," she whispered into my ear. "From now and until the end of my days, no matter what becomes of me, you'll have nothing to fear. You have my word. What is inside me will *never* have you."

When she pulled back from our embrace, I looked into her teary eyes. "Nikki..."

"I wish there was more I could give you, Clara. There must be something I can do to protect you. But after yesterday, I doubt that I'll be allowed to stay in the castle for much longer. For right now, Elliott struggles with his clouded priorities..."

She turned away sadly. "I came to help him and protect you. But it can be such trouble to keep myself thinking logically. I fear that he will either have me destroyed or cast out."

"Let me talk to him."

She smiled faintly. "No, it's too late for that."

Before I could try to refute that, a movement caught my eye. I turned to see the approaching—

"Wilhelm?"

"Well, if it isn't little miss human," the guard wistfully greeted me with a little bow. "And as it turns out, Lady Craven is still here! As pretty as she is *utterly* insane..."

I winced nervously at his questionable choice of compliment, but Nikki grinned lovingly at him. It didn't particularly surprise me anymore that she could accept offhanded remarks like that with a sense of fondness and ownership. *Nikki might be insane, or she might not be. There might not even be a real answer. But she's certainly* **complicated...**

Wilhelm turned to me cheerily. "Apparently, your immediate presence has been requested in the throne room. Seems to be rather urgent..."

"Really? Now?" I glanced at Nikki.

"Go," she smirked. "I'll be fine without you."

"Actually..." Wilhelm mischievously glanced to her. "Your sticking around has saved me a fair bit of wandering. Dreadfully boring, hunting you folks down, and you might know how much I *hate* boring... anyway! As it so turns out, he's looking for you as well. Didn't say why, just that the two of you had some... talking to do."

It was such a faint movement that you'd have missed

it with a blink, but Nikki's lip just slightly twitched with a frown.

<hr>

WHEN WE ARRIVED, ELLIOTT WASN'T ACTUALLY sitting in the throne. Curiously, he was standing in front of it, his arms crossed as he studied it from afar. If I didn't know any better, it was as if he were figuring out if he deserved it...

He wasn't the only one in the room. Besides a few guards, Lorelei and Sebastian were here too. They glanced up as Nikki, Wilhelm, and I arrived.

"Clara," he turned to face me. "I'm really sorry for running off earlier from dinner. I had to be alone to think on things..."

"I know," I smiled warmly. "What's up?"

Lorelei and Sebastian shared a forlorn glance, and I felt the first stings of fear. Something was wrong; it was written all over Elliott's face...

"Did you notice the moon tonight?"

I frowned. "Of course I did. It's as beautiful as it always is here. Your skies make the whole night sky look phenomenal."

He smiled sadly. "For the last couple of days, there's been an alignment. It grants a great and powerful boost to certain kinds of magic. Even old and difficult spells..."

The vampire lord paused; his pained expression filled me with dread.

"Elliott, what are you saying?"

His eyes sadly locked onto mine.

"Clara, there is a way to send you back to your world. And it has to be tonight."

28

ELLIOTT

She didn't make a move.

There wasn't even a peep out of her as she just stood there, watching me silently. That was the hardest part – the fact that I couldn't read her.

Of course, I could read everybody else. Lorelei and Sebastian were upset, and my sister quickly became a violent mixture of fear and hatred. I ignored all of their looks, focusing on the only one in the room that mattered.

I didn't need any kind of increased perception to grasp her reaction. Clara struggled with this news, and it was written cleanly across her face. What I'd just told her was forcing her to decide which world she really wanted to stay in. If I were in her position, there wasn't a shadow of a doubt that I'd grapple with the weight of that choice.

Even to me, it seemed deeply unfair. I had the fortune of centuries at my back, and the luxury of nearby family and practical advisors.

At the end of the day, Clara Blackwell was just a seventeen-year-old girl – a human, here from another world. In everything that I'd seen out of her so far, in her forgiveness and her unending cheeriness, she was so capable of fantastic things; but she was still a child, and a fearful one.

"Clara."

Almost in a daze, she looked at me.

"I think you should go back."

The effect was immediate. Devastation was plastered across her gorgeous face as she blinked, her lips trembling under the weight of powerful and tragic emotions.

"You... you think that I..."

"Clara." I steeled my resolve, pushing down every last painful reaction in my heart and soul. "Even if I could somehow promise you'd never be attacked within this castle again, I cannot protect you from the retribution of the Eight Holds. The vampire lords will come for you, and I can only keep them at bay for so long."

My beautiful Clara looked destroyed.

I felt the sting of a tear and fought it back.

"I have to be honest with you. If you choose to stay here, Clara, you will be in constant danger for the rest of your life."

I was killing something inside of her. It was plain across her face; every last, bitter ounce that I pushed down on that emotional weight stung me harder than any pain I'd ever felt before.

She didn't move a muscle, even as tears began to stream down her face. "I don't want to go."

If I showed any weakness or empathy, I knew I'd lose the strength to do this. I had to be strong for her, to help her make the right decision. But I couldn't stop myself from recognizing the single most powerful thought in my heart, the thing I wanted more than anything to tell her:

I don't want you to leave me.

Instead, I replied: "Clara Blackwell, when you perish because I couldn't protect you, everything you love inside me will die with you."

It took the last ounce of resistance I had to say the words, no matter how true they might have been. *I'm being cruel to be kind,* I reminded myself. The painful irony of this choice twisted the knife in my spirit ever harder.

I felt my resolve collapsing. There wasn't any more strength left inside me, and I knew then, all of a sudden: *No. I can't do this. I'll find a way, there has to be another way...*

As I opened my mouth to beg her to stay...

Clara painfully averted her eyes, unable to look at me. "Please, just let me have one last time to see everything I'm giving up."

My world came crashing down, and it was my own

fault. But she'd spoken the words, and there was no denying the truth of what I'd said.

You're safer on your own world.

And thus I resigned myself to my fate.

"Very well then," I heard myself lifelessly say. "You have free reign of the castle for one hour... but on one condition."

Clara met my stare. Her eyes were just as dead inside as mine. "What's the condition?"

My sister stood still in such a violent vacuum of emotion that I couldn't read her any longer. But this was insignificant to me as I leveled my gaze at her, letting her see my fury.

"Witness the punishment of Nikki Craven."

⁂

FEELING THE EYES OF EVERY PERSON IN THE ROOM ON me, I silently ascended the stairs and took my place on the throne.

The doors opened. Asarra and Viktor stepped into the room, freezing in place when they sensed the hanging air of complete solemnity. I waved them over to Wilhelm; one look at his mirthless expression, and they didn't have to ask.

"Nikki Craven, step forward."

Terror flicked across her face, but she did as I told

her. My sister broke away from the group and approached the throne, stopping just a few steps back from the first stair.

"Kneel," I ordered her.

Nikki defiantly tilted her head. "You want me to kneel? Are you being serious right now?"

My voice boomed as I rose up from my seat.

"*KNEEL BEFORE YOUR LORD!*"

I didn't care how much trembling fear or quiet horror I felt in every vampire in the room. There was no patience left in me for her madness; I refused to entertain her any longer.

My sister looked like a child then, lost and alone, as she dropped to a knee in front of me. Her eyes welled with tears.

"Nikki Craven, you are guilty of endangering the life of a guest of the royal family. You have, in your insanity and foolishness, put one of the most valuable lives on the planet in jeopardy." I shook my head in complete defeat. "The first human ever seen on Earth, and you try to take her away? Do you have even the *slightest grasp* of what could have happened to her? What could happen to this kingdom if the other holds learn she was nearly ripped out of this castle by a sleeper agent?"

My sister remained silent, but her eyes said it all. So did her heart. She knew what she had done, and the dangers she'd gambled to do it.

"I will not execute my last remaining sibling," I told her, lifting my gaze to the troubled Lorelei. "If our own mother didn't have you slain for the things that you've already done, then killing now would only show us all that she was *wrong*."

The room went deathly silent.

Clara clearly couldn't take much more of this; before she could voice objections, Lorelei clasped her hand onto the human's shoulder and silently shook her head. While Clara lowered her gaze to the floor, Lorelei turned away, unable to watch.

"Brother..." Nikki sadly murmured. All traces of her madness were gone for the time being, and her haunted gaze stayed glued to the bottom stair. "I just want you to know... that I accept whatever wrath you feel. Punish me however you desire." In complete regret, she lifted her eyes to meet my own. "I love you, Brother."

I read her heart. I believed her.

And it changed nothing.

"Nikki Craven, with all the powers vested in me as the vampire lord of Stonehold, I strip you of all royalty privileges and your rightful place in Stonehold Castle. Henceforth, you are denounced by the Crown, forever and always. From now 'til the day you die, you are a Craven in name only."

Nobody said a word. They didn't have to.

I could *feel* their horror and shame.

"I humbly accept your mercy," Nikki replied. "You don't want me in your life anymore. I know. I understand. Let me grab my few things, and I'll be gone from the Isle of Obsidian for eternity." She started to climb to her feet.

I shook my head. "I didn't order you to rise."

Nikki looked confused.

"Kneel," I commanded again.

She slumped back into position.

"My gaze slid across the room. I read all of their resignation and confusion, their sorrow and fear. The only heart I cared to read was Clara's, and yet I would always be blind to her emotions.

My stare focused on my disgraced sister.

"Without your efforts, the traitorous Sabine would have taken Clara far away to distant lands. You and I both know I'd have never found her again. For the remainder of my life, I would have become a gnarled creature of regret and shame; with my failure, Stonehold would descend into an era of despair and ruination."

Rising from my throne, I walked down to the bottom step and reached for my hip. I unsheathed my ceremonial sword and withdrew it from its scabbard. I stared down into her surprised eyes as I planted it onto her shoulder beside her throat.

"Nikki Craven, for your selfless bravery and valor, I hereby appoint you my vassal, with all the duties and privileges of such. Now and forever, you will serve as guardian of the Crown, personal advisor to the reigning vampire lord... and you will remain my valued, constant companion."

I might have expected relief. What I saw in her eyes instead was a powerful love and respect. She lowered her face. "I live to serve, Brother."

"Rise, my vassal."

The sword tip lifted from her throat, and I sheathed it. Nikki threw her arms around me in a firm embrace, and I couldn't resist a smug smile. Besides, she wouldn't see it... but then, when I noticed the rest of the room silently watching me, it disappeared from my face with a scowl.

I pulled from her embrace. The sanctity of the moment had almost made me forget my reasons for choosing to do this now, and I felt my heart break as I turned to the human among us.

"An hour from now, join us in the pavilion. You'll have your moment to say your goodbyes to everyone, and we'll send you back to your world."

Clara didn't say a word as she turned and left.

Viktor and Assara shared a solemn, knowing glance, and they turned to me. At my silent nod, Wilhelm joined them as they left after her. After all, she had been in danger before...

When they were gone, I turned my back and faced

the looming throne. As tonight slowly drew to its end, there was so much left to do. Part of me feared what tomorrow would bring, and that was perfectly fine.

It was best to let myself feel the fear now, to contemplate and suffer it. I could let myself feel weakness now, to become intimately aware of my shortcomings and grave disappointment. I would let it all run its course. Tonight was for suffering, for bathing myself in pain and heartbreak.

But tomorrow was a different day.

I would wake up strong. I would make myself prepared to do what must be done, no matter how difficult, all for the good of the hold.

"Lord Elliott," Sebastian broke the silence. "No disrespect, but I have to ask – why did you make up the part about the moon? This great 'cosmic alignment' you spoke of... none of that was true."

Nikki turned to me in complete disbelief.

Ignoring her judgment, I replied calmly.

"I didn't lie to her before: tonight's my only chance to do this. Come the rising sun, I know I won't be strong enough to make this choice again. Clara Blackwell must be protected at any cost, even if doing so means that we lose the chance at something truly powerful together..."

When I turned away, it hid my face. I couldn't stand letting any of them see the pain in my eyes as I felt my heart shatter.

29

CLARA

The guards stood at full attention as I passed by – on Elliott's orders, they allowed me total access to nearly everything in sight.

The Knightly Trio followed me at a distance. I wandered around the castle, taking in the décor. My feet marched me down hallways and corridors as I looked over beautiful magnificence that I was doomed to never see again.

As I wandered, I even came across the old, forgotten bookcase against the wall that had very nearly sealed my fate, merely three weeks before.

I planted my palm against the aged, warped wood. It was cool to the touch, cool and gnarled against my trembling fingers. "You know, I never thought I'd ever miss you… but here we are."

Asarra gave me a look.

"Behind here is the abandoned wing," I said.

"...Yes," she nodded slowly. "How would you know about that, Clara?"

"It's where I woke up," I sadly answered.

"Really?" Wilhelm asked. "It was *here?*"

"The bookcase here was just ajar enough for me to get out," I continued. "If not for that little gap, I would have stayed trapped in the wing... I'd have died of starvation back there."

"How awful," Viktor noted.

"I woke up on the cold stone ground, near a bunch of books and vials," I recalled fondly. "Then I clamoured out and searched my way out. Must have taken me an hour to find this exit..."

"That's when I found you," Asarra remembered.

"Heh. Not before I spent a couple of hours hiding. The servants looked so strange at first, prowling around with their pale skin and sharp features... I suspected the worst and kept out of sight. When you captured me, I'd been creeping stealthily along the halls for a while..."

"You suspected right!" Wilhelm chuckled. It had been a while since I'd heard him laugh, and I knew I'd miss the sound. "Knowing what we all do now, any of those poor servants would have uncontrollably bled you dry on *sight* for your blood."

"Yeah... good thing you found me," I glanced up at Asarra. "Don't think I ever thanked you."

"It is I who should thank you," she replied, as stoic as ever. "As a guard, we hate boredom. These last few weeks with you have been anything but."

"I'm happy to hear it," I grinned. "Know how you can repay me for that, right now?

"How?" Viktor asked.

Asarra tilted her head. "Say the word, Clara."

My mind filled with beautiful memories of that otherworldly sky. "Lead me outside."

NIGHT HAD FALLEN.

I took the time to walk out towards the courtyard, appreciating the gardens under those beautiful stars. The sweet aroma of lush flowers greeted me as I wandered the hedges, taking deep breaths of foreign flora as I took in that deep, unending cosmos above.

Once I had spent my fill with the grand gardens, I laid down in the springy grass for my last chance at stargazing their night sky. As I tried to fight away a great and looming sadness, I did my best to commit the sprawling, stunning abyss to memory: studying every last one of its cosmic colors, sweeping lights, and radiant stars.

On my back beneath that universe, I cried.

I don't know how long I lied there until I felt a tap on my shoulder. I nodded; after all, I knew who it was.

"It's time." Wilhelm spoke regretfully.

He offered his hand. I took it, pulling up to my feet and dusting myself off. Viktor and Assara stood quietly beside him, both watching me with pain in their eyes. As I quietly walked past them, she pulled a handkerchief from a pocket and gave it to me; I dabbed at my eyes and wiped away the sadness.

"Thank you, Asarra."

For the first time that I could remember, the knight smiled. "My pleasure, Clara."

My eyes turned to the distant pavilion, with the handkerchief tightly held in my fist. I could still see the top of it above the hedges; the path forward lied there before me. Every step towards the pavilion filled my heart with depression and dread, but I knew it had to be done. At least I had the knightly trio there with me, fanned out and taking every step alongside me in silent support. As our group quietly wound between thick walls of unimaginable beauty, the four of us walked this path with solemn, heavy hearts.

I was grateful to not have to do it alone.

The trail was over far too quickly. I stood at the edge of the platform, afraid to go forward. The others were already here: Sebastian, Lorelei, and Nikki stood gathered in the center, while Elliott quietly brooded just a little ways off.

A gloved, armored hand caringly settled onto my shoulder. I could feel myself begin to crumble inside, but before it could work its way out, Wilhelm whispered into my ear. "We won't leave you, little miss human. Look to us if you need to."

I nodded silently, wiping away my tears with Assara's gift. Realizing I still had it, I tried to hand it back to her; she merely shook her head.

"Keep it and remember us, Clara."

I tucked it into my pocket and threw my arms around Wilhelm. "Oof!" He humored me. "What a powerful grip you've got there! We should have made you a guard too..."

His lighthearted chuckle gave me the smile I so desperately needed. I turned to the others, and hugged Viktor as well ("It's been a pleasure, little Clara"). When it came time for Assara, she looked uncomfortable, but held out her hand awkwardly. I smiled sadly and shook it; she surprised me by pulling me into a light hug, fondly tapping the top of my head with her palm a few times, and then pulling away again.

The others had noticed me by now, and were waving me over. Wilhelm lightly placed a palm to my back and coerced me forward, and I walked up onto the pavilion and towards my destiny.

30

CLARA

As I stepped forwards, I noticed some hasty chalk markings all over the ground. *I guess that answers the question of who's performing the spell...*

Nikki and Sebastian paused in their hushed chatter, watching me with a collective sadness. I barely noticed them as I walked up to Elliott, who turned and faced me with a solemn expression.

"Is this how it ends?" I asked bleakly.

For a moment, I thought I saw a small flicker of regret across his face. But it was relatively dark, and the moment was gone before I could be sure.

"I don't want you to go. But you have to."

My head lowered.

His fingers came into view; he lifted my chin with the tip of one, forcing me to see his dark and handsome stare. In those radiant eyes, I saw so many things. As I studied them, I felt his remorse, his longing, his fear and his uncertainty.

But I also felt his resolve, and I smiled sadly. *Elliott hates this, just as much as I do. But he's doing what he thinks is best.*

I planted a small kiss on his lips.

He didn't fight it; he gave into the feeling.

"It's now or never," he whispered to me.

"How about 'never'?"

Elliott smiled despondently. "If only."

The deepest pangs of misery yet struck at my heart, like whipping waves in a storm at sea. With heavy spirits, I turned away from him and walked up to Nikki and Sebastian.

"How is this happening?"

The elderly sage placed a comforting hand on my shoulder. "Very shortly, Lady Craven will be performing a rather ancient and forgotten spell. The process is similar to before. Come, stand over here..." He guided me towards the center of the pavilion, but I hesitated, glancing at Lorelei.

"Wait," I resisted his push. "Won't I have the time to say proper goodbyes?"

"You will have an opportunity before you go," he reassured me. "For now, we need to make the first preparations. Please, if you'd kindly..."

Dejectedly, I followed his lead. Sebastian had me stop

in the same spot as before, and I glanced around the open, curved pillars of the courtyard pavilion before facing that incredibly night sky one last time.

"Focus, please."

With a heavy sigh, I lowered my gaze.

"Lord Craven, whenever you're ready."

Nikki strolled towards me with the spell-book held open in her hand. She stopped right in front to slide her finger down the page, taking another moment to properly study the ancient text. "Now that we're aware of your inherent resilience to magic, we can compensate for that..."

"Is that what the sigils are for?"

The vampire vassal smiled crookedly. "What? No. That's because I'm not a sorceress, duh. Are you kidding? I mean, if you wanted me to try this *without* them, well... let's just say the results could be gruesome." Her face tellingly lit up. "In fact, you know what? I think I quite like that idea. We can ditch the sigils and try this spell the old-fashioned way, but I can't really guarantee that *all* of you would make it..." Her radiant eyes sparked with deviance. "How attached are you to your skin, by the way? Let's say, a scale of one to ten..."

By now, I'd gotten so used to her playful madness that I just smiled and shook my head. "Nikki, I *need* my skin," I reminded her. "I can't have you just banishing it to another world!"

She shrugged cheerfully. "Oh well. Thought I'd try. Thought maybe you'd be reasonable..." The warmth gradually faded from her face as she held her place in the book with a finger and drew me into a heavy embrace. "I think I'm gonna miss you, little snack."

"I think I'll miss you too." I patted her back affectionately. "Hey, you remember that one time that you kidnapped me to prove a point?"

Nikki stiffened. "...Rings a bell."

"Yeah," I chuckled. "Let's *never* do that again."

As we pulled away, I couldn't tell how much of her grin was due to madness or amusement. In her mind, they were probably one and the same.

Her smile gradually fell as her serious side took the spotlight. It was probably for the best; there was no telling what would happen if she descended into playful wickedness in the middle of casting the spell. "It's time, Clara."

Feeling glum inside, I knew she was right.

Nikki stepped back and pointed out the sigils. "I don't have a formal education. My talents were refined by renegade mages in the wild, so I lack a lot of basic fundamentals. That's what these are all for. Think of these sigils like shields, bouncing the spell right to this point. They'll focus the wild magic; they'll target it to whomever stands where you are now and greatly amplify it. All of this will *probably* overcome your resistance, but I don't think that this spell will ever work on you again."

"Well then, I guess I'll count myself lucky that it's a one-way trip." I muttered despondently.

She either ignored or didn't hear my self-pity. "For now, stay where you are. After I activate the sigils and begin the spell, you will have a chance to say goodbye to everyone while I charge it. But I can't start without a target in place."

I nodded morosely. "Okay."

With my consent granted, Nikki turned away, flipped the spell-book to the right page, and began walking towards the others. "I need you three in position. Mother, come here; Sebastian, over here; Elliott, stand there."

Silently, they assumed their spots at different corners and turned to me. Elliott was to my left, Lorelei to my right, and Sebastian stood behind. Their grim faces told me that they, just like me, didn't want to be any part of this.

Nikki stood in front, finishing the diamond of vampires around me. She lifted the book up high in front and lightly tossed it, clicking the fingers of both hands simultaneously. As with Sabine, the tome levitated before her in a light glow.

With that same rolling motion of her wrists over one

another, she clicked both sets of fingers one after the other...

The sigils all beamed to life around us.

As the pavilion brightened in a powerful, heavenly glow, the three stunned knights quietly watched from the sidelines. They all turned to me and offered various smiles and encouragement.

"Focus," Nikki reminded me. "Eyes forward."

It was clear that she was straining under the power of these sigils. She collapsed to a knee, both palms against the ground, and the others quickly voiced their concerns. "I'm... fine!" She snapped in a grunt, resisting what looked like an invisible gravitation pull. Nikki gradually climbed back to her feet, bracing herself against the power of the sigils. "I just... need to... *concentrate*..."

Back upright, she thrust out her palms to me. With her eyes glued to the pages of the floating tome, Nikki began chanting in a bizarre, magical tongue. Every so often, one of the sigils around us would sound off a musical note while flickering to a different color.

The intensity of the spell was taking a visible toll on her; biased or not, I almost wanted to tell her to call the entire thing off.

With one final, strained sentence, a powerful breeze roared through the pavilion. Nikki relaxed her power stance and gazed at her hands, flexing all of her fingers.

"It's safe now," she called out. "Only Clara can move –

the rest of you have to stay in place." Nikki glanced at me. "This is your time for goodbyes..."

I didn't have to be told twice.

First, I whirled around and raced to Sebastian. "I didn't know you much, and I'm sorry. You seem like a kind and wise old guy."

The sage beamed. "It's wonderful to hear that from fellow vampires, but from a *human?*" He side-eyed me affectionately. "Now that's the kind of praise I'll keep until the grave."

Sebastian held out his arms. I turned to Nikki for approval. When she nodded with a grin, I sank into his warm embrace. "Please take care of Elliott for me," I whispered in his ear.

"Consider his ongoing health and wisdom my parting gift to you." At those words, I kissed him on the cheek.

Next, I approached Lorelei.

"You're rather interesting, for a human," she observed aloofly. "Such a feisty spirit. No doubt, you'd have made a *fine* vampire." Lorelei reached for me and planted a light kiss on my forehead. It felt cool to the touch, yet filled with endearment. "Such a pity it is to lose you, little one."

"You too, Your Royal Highness."

"Hah!" She chuckled heartily. "The manners again. I'd nearly forgotten how polite you are..." The matronly vampire leaned forward to whisper in my ear. "When you die in your world, Clara, do me a favor and get yourself born here, if you can. I may only have a century or two left, so don't take your time..."

"I'll get right on that," I smiled sadly.

I ran up to Nikki, who merely gave me a bored glance. "We already had our moment, little snack. Go bother Elliott. He'd appreciate the time more."

I gave her a quick, hearty hug and ran up to the man from my dreams. His forlorn eyes were filled with such sorrow that I could barely meet their gaze.

"Guess this is it," I muttered sadly.

Elliott watched me for a moment, his sadness just as deep and meaningful as mine. "I will never be the same without you, Clara Blackwell."

I lifted my face. "Do you really mean that?"

He nodded solemnly. "Of course I do."

We both knew that there wasn't much time, but clearly neither of us knew what to say or do in our last moments together. Giving in to instinct, I knew I needed to feel his touch one last time. My arms flung around him as I cried into his chest. One of his hands disappeared into my thick hair, the other slid onto my back, and the vampire lord clutched my body close to his own.

I heard him murmur, but I couldn't hear.

"Didn't catch that," I whispered, looking up.

Elliott smiled handsomely, and the magical breeze whipped lightly at his brunette curls.

"I said 'I love you, Clara Blackwell.'"

His lips descended upon mine.

We were pulled into such a powerful kiss that I felt every heartstring inside tenderly sing. I felt that kiss down to my toes, pouring love into every vein in my body. I'd never kissed a boy before. But it didn't matter; I knew in that moment that no other boy, no matter *what* world they came from, could *ever* kiss me like this again.

"Time's running out," Nikki called to us.

He and I pulled out of the embrace. "I love you too, Elliott Craven," I whispered in his ear, leaving a small peck there. "Until the day I die."

"Until the day I die," he repeated with a smile.

Before Nikki could get angrier, I sadly walked over to my position and stood facing her. "Okay. I'm ready," I lied to her as I fought back my tears.

She meaningfully lifted her palms up again, holding them out towards me. "Alright, everyone, you heard our little human... I need all of you to visualize her now... picture her in your minds, as sharply as you can... visualize Clara as you see her now, bathed in a bright, green light..."

The others stiffened their posture and stared at me. "Concentrate," she ordered the others. "I can't do it alone. Cast lingering thoughts aside, all of you, and *focus on the human!*"

All the sigils began to hum in a united chorus,

glowing a spectrum of rainbow colors together. Nikki grunted under their magical intensity and almost buckled again, but kept her stance. "You're doing great!" She growled. "Keep it up!"

Startlingly, a small crackle of green lightning briefly buzzed in my face. Another came near a hand, then another at my feet, one from behind...

All of a sudden, a circle snapped to life at my feet, glowed up a green pillar of light around me. My first spell or not, I was just as awed as before as I trailed my fingers within the bright column. I watched how my movements caused subtle gaps in the light, and how quickly they disappeared.

"Good!" Nikki gasped under the strain. "Don't lose that image in your head! I need you all to keep up the barrier as I cast this!"

She withdrew her palms and held them up to the stars, chanting at the top of her lungs. Around us, the wind kicked into overdrive, billowing all of our clothes like a tropical storm.

I quietly watched how she started powerfully glowing under the night sky. With the intensity of her recitation, Nikki pulled into her body the beginnings of an incredible strength. It was so far beyond what I'd seen enter Sabine that I suddenly grew afraid of it.

The moment confronted me, then and there:

This is really happening. I'm being sent away.

Before I could blurt out a desperate plea, I felt my attention drawn to Elliott. He stood there, the unending pain scribbled across his face. His heart was shattering and there was nothing I could do to save either of us.

Nikki screamed in pain.

My gaze snapped back to her. In the instant, she brought her palms down and hurled the light inside her towards me.

As I fell backwards, the last thing that I saw was Elliott Craven, diving desperately toward me. But my body never hit the stone; when I struck where the pavilion's floor should be, the world all around me exploded into an abyss of impossible beauty. I found myself plummeting downward, at the comforting whim of intoxicating, bursting galaxies, swirling lights, and endless time...

※

WHEN I SLOWLY CAME TO, I FELT GRASSY MUD AGAINST my face and hands, and the disgusting lapping of water up to my waist.

My eyes gradually opened.

The daylight bothered me. I groaned with a headache as I started to pull myself forward. With sluggish movements, I dragged my body out from the horrid sensations of slapping, rolling water over my legs.

When I crawled free and sank down into dry land, I

took a deep breath and rolled myself over. As my eyes slowly adjusted to the sunlight, I held a hand up to shield them. Everything miserably hurt, and I was apparently left out in the open.

The light grew easier to manage. I found the strength to keep my eyes open, and peered across the dim, drowning whiteness at my environment.

Apparently, I was at the edge of a huge lake, soaking wet from my stomach down. Confused, I drifted my gaze down to my unfamiliar clothes, wondering why I wasn't in a school uniform.

"Oh yeah," I muttered to myself as memories slowly drifted back. "Wonder if vampiric fabrics are dry clean only..."

Comprehension dawned on me, just in time to hear an elderly voice as a caretaker stumbled into view. "Oi! Whatcha doing way out here, little lady, you having a swim in the lake?"

He paused, kneeling to get a good look at me. "Wait just a second! Why, I reckon you look just like that missing girl... are you, what was her name... *Clara Blackwell?*"

Disoriented, I reached to my throat and felt the chain of a black necklace, with a red ruby inset. *My grandmother's,* I remembered. It was dry and warm to the touch. It even felt as if the metal were throbbing.

"Yes," I muttered groggily. "I think I am..."

31

THE UNKNOWN

Thousands of miles away from Clara Blackwell, elevator doors opened on the fiftieth floor of a skyscraper. An unfailingly polite young man in business casual attire stepped out into a carpeted corporate hallway. The man wore a cheery smile on his face as he adjusted his horn-rimmed glasses, then brushed away brunette curls from the lenses.

Nestled in the crook of his arm was a featureless binder that, were it to be unceremoniously dropped onto the international black market, would have gone for bids that rival the GDP of small nations.

This man did not crave power.

He was content enough to protect it.

He knew that power was a very fickle thing. Once it was yours, it became difficult to maintain; too many of his betters had chased it, only to be destroyed by their own incapability to know when to release it. Power consumed and destroyed them—and that was a path this man chose to never walk.

What he enjoyed most was to serve those who knew how to consolidate and defend it.

The man strolled along the office corridor, eyes strictly to the front with his infectious smile. Respectfully, he gave a quiet nod to the few others he passed on his way. Some were workers, briefly given access to this floor to perform some brief, menial task or another. Most of them were other executive assistants, forced to scurry around to meet the revolving whims of upper management.

His polished shoes took him around two corners before he came to the door of his master. The executive assistant gave a polite knock, and he awaited further orders. Once he'd heard a command from inside the room, the man quietly stepped into the office of the Chief Operations Director for Clover Pharmaceutical.

Embroiled in a phone call, Vera Partridge barely paid any mind to him. He could see that she was deep in her element – her eyes were like those of a viper, her voice deceptively sultry, yet laced with poison. As her most trusted servant, he was allowed access to her office for her corporate politics; quietly closing the door on his way in, the man patiently leaned back against the wall until she was ready, clutching the featureless binder in both arms against his chest.

The widowed Mrs. Partridge ended the call with a pleasant tone that hid her utter contempt. Pinching the bridge of her nose, she sighed quietly before composing herself.

Her snakelike eyes turned to him.

"There you are..." she feigned sweetness in her smile. "I find myself *dangerously* low on good news... what do you have for me this time?"

Her assistant nodded once.

"There's been a vision."

"A vision?" Her smile fell, and she sat straight up in her chair with an intent stare. He always admired her most when she was all business. "Tell me what you know."

The man tapped the binder in his arms. "The vision comes from one of our higher level seers. It was reportedly strong enough that two others have given similar, albeit murkier, accounts."

"Interesting..." Her eyes narrowed intensely. "What was content of this vision?"

The assistant couldn't resist smiling. "There's been a traveler. Completed a cycle, back and forth. It seems a rift has opened."

Vera Partridge's posture instantly stiffened at his

words as she stoically lowered her gaze upon him. Her question was simple: "Where?"

"Europe," he casually replied.

Pensively tenting her fingers, she leaned back in her executive chair. "The ancient records all suggest two gateways in present-day Europe: one in Romania, and one in England."

Her assistant merely nodded in agreement. "The seer, unfortunately, could not quite clarify. The first-hand account details the experience as fleeting, yet quite overwhelming."

"Where is this seer now?"

"Medical wing. Comatose."

Vera locked eyes with him. "But you extracted an interview with her?"

"Him," he subtly corrected, "and yes."

"How did you manage that?"

The assistant smiled noncommittally. "Well, the few visions we have on record always seemed clearest while the experience was at its freshest."

She narrowed her eyes. "Go on."

Noncommittally, he shrugged. "Since seers are not *generally* in an agreeable position during this time, I had all his sedation completely withheld during all the cooldown procedures until I learned what I needed to…"

Her face changed.

The man paused, smiling offhandedly. "Oh, don't

look at me like that. The doctors all assure me that they have him stable now. He'll probably even be fine. If he survives the ordeal, he'll be back upright in his chair, ready to work again in two to three weeks' time."

He stepped forward, reaching into his button-up pocket to place a small audio playback device on the counter. "But more importantly, you'll find everything you need to know right here."

As he took a couple of steps back, Vera's eyes flickered from the device to his face. Even with him, she was skilled at hiding or fabricating her emotions until the right moment.

For the most part, he actually appreciated her ambiguity; it kept him sharp, quick on his feet.

"As always, you never disappoint." His boss smiled with great affection, "You have done *very* well. Thank you."

He modestly nodded. "I aim to serve."

She kept her smile, reflecting on the great many times that he'd proven those words right, all in the four years since she had chosen him.

"Leave. I'll update you as necessary."

Mrs. Partridge watched him politely leave the room. Once she was alone again, she considered the implications of the seer's vision.

With barely any magic on Earth, it was a tremendous

surprise that such a powerful burst of clairvoyance struck one of the few still capable of receiving it.

And a long-lost rift, at that...

Without wasting time, she clicked the device in her hand and listened to the twelve minutes of coherent audio. By the time the seer's incoherent screaming overcame the playback, Vera Partridge had heard everything that she needed to.

She lifted the landline phone at her desk and dialed a number. After a few rings, the connection clicked, and a voice on the other end of the line responded.

"Vera?"

"It's time to activate Project Layers," Vera Partridge spoke with the calm and collected restraint of a national chess grandmaster. "There has been a vision. I think we've just found another Earth..."

Are you ready to find out what happens next in Clara and Elliot's story?

A Witch Between Worlds #3: The Witch's Reunion is available NOW! Find it on Amazon today!

I HOPE YOU LOVE IT!

A Witch Between Worlds Series
Season #1 (Books #1-#10 is complete!)

Here's the reading order:

The Vampire's Witch (Book 1)
Trials of the Vampire (Book 2) Available Now
A Witch's Reunion (Book 3) Available Now
The Witch's Dilemma (Book 4) Available Now
The Witch's Peril (Book 5) Available Now

The Witch's Path (Book 6) Available Now
The Witch's Kiss (Book 7) Available Now
The Witch's Heart (Book 8) Available Now
The Witch's Sorrow (Book 9) Available Now
The Witch's Destiny (Book 10) Available Now!

Look for Season 2 of A Witch Between Worlds starting February 2019!

The Witch's Wolf (Book 11) Available February 2019

Made in the USA
Columbia, SC
13 December 2019